ILLUSTRATED   S,
ood-engraving, have added so muc
it was customary for publishers
nd expensive plates of those even
h general attention from the publi
n the King's Collection and in tl
itish Museum). Amongst the mo
of which we this week give a cop
icture," several other delineations
; one showing Old London-bridg
asses of ice; another looking alor
facing the Temple was called. I
, and many other sports going fo
Thames was frozen over at Londor
rkable circumstance took place.
e are, in the collections to which v
ks on the river and in the park

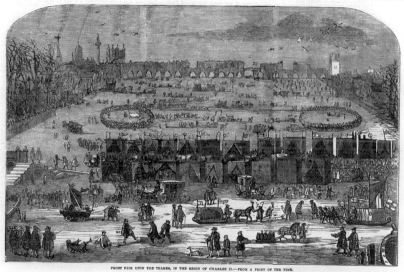

FROST FAIR UPON THE THAMES, IN THE REIGN OF CHARLES II.—FROM A PRINT OF THE TIME.

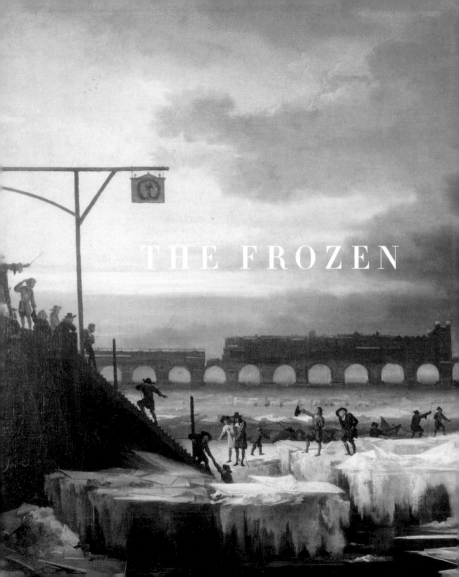

THE FROZEN

Helen Humphreys

THAMES

Delacorte Press

THE FROZEN THAMES
A Delacorte Press Book

PUBLISHING HISTORY
McClelland and Stewart hardcover edition published
in Canada in October 2007
Delacorte Press edition / January 2009

Published by Bantam Dell
A Division of Random House, Inc.
New York, New York

Book design by CS Richardson

Delacorte Press is a registered trademark of Random House, Inc.,
and the colophon is a trademark of Random House, Inc.

Library of Congress Cataloging in Publication Data
Humphreys, Helen, 1961-
The frozen Thames / Helen Humphreys.
p. cm.
ISBN 978-0-385-34281-0
1. Thames River (England)--Fiction. I. Title.
PR9199.3.H822F76 2009
813'.54--dc22
2008032356

Printed in China

www.bantamdell.com

SCH   10 9 8 7 6 5 4 3 2 1

In its long history, the river Thames
has frozen solid forty times.

These are the stories of that frozen river.

1142

Matilda is under siege. For more than three months now she's been barricaded inside this castle in Oxford while her cousin, Stephen, circles the ramparts with his men, waits for slow starvation to force her out and into his capture.

They have eaten all the horses and burnt all the furniture. They have retreated through pockets of cold, to a small room without windows at the base of the tower. At night they huddle together like dogs.

Matilda is Queen of England, but her cousin has stolen the Crown, and now she is locked into battle with him. She has been locked into battle with him for almost seven years.

Stephen would never have been able to race to London to claim the Crown if Matilda had been in England at the time, not stranded in France with her child husband, Geoffrey of Anjou, who everyone agreed had descended from the daughter of Satan. She would never have had to marry a fourteen-year-old if her brother, William, had lived, instead of drowning in the Channel in 1120 on the White Ship, rowed across by drunken men who, in their drunkenness, hit a rock and holed the boat. Their father, Henry I, King of England, was so grief-stricken that he never smiled again, and decided to pass on the throne to his daughter, Matilda, even though it was unheard of for a woman to inherit the Crown and govern the realm.

Matilda would never have had to think about being Queen if her father hadn't died suddenly. Her father wouldn't have died suddenly if he'd listened to everyone around him and not eaten such a huge helping of stewed lamprey eels.

It is night at Oxford Castle. Usually Matilda makes the rounds, visits her men slouched by the narrow windows, their longbows leaned up against the stone, but tonight she is too weary, cannot think of anything appropriate to cheer them further onwards in her service, towards their very deaths, so she goes instead into the interior of the castle to find her maid, who will prepare her for sleep.

Her maid, Jane, is not in the room at the base of the tower. Matilda finds her out in the courtyard, staring up at the sky, Matilda's nightshirt slung over her arm.

"Look, ma'am," she says, as soon as she sees the Queen. "It's snowing."

So it is. Big, lacy flakes that swim down out of the darkness decorate the shoulders of the Queen's maid.

"Ma'am," says Jane. "The snow is the same colour as your nightshirt."

Matilda takes her three strongest knights. They

make a rope out of their leggings and they wait until the hour is the darkest, the snow is the thickest. They are lowered to the ground from one of the castle windows by the men they have left behind. All four of them are dressed in nightshirts and they move like ghosts, softly and slowly, towards the edge of the river.

The Thames is frozen. Matilda saw it freeze. These days and days of the siege, she has spent a good deal of time looking out at the enemy camped on the edge of the river. A week ago the temperature dropped, and now Stephen's men walk up and down the ice on horseback. They have even built two fires there, near the shore.

In order to get to the other side of the river, Matilda and her three men will have to walk between those signal fires. They move in single file, a man in front, then Matilda, two men behind her. They move slowly and carefully, do not speak, keep close together.

Through the swirling snow, Matilda can see the glow of the fires, can hear the voices of Stephen's army. If they can just pass between those fires they will cross to the middle of the river, out past the sentries, and from there they can walk to the other side. Matilda is equally opposed and equally supported by the people of Britain, and there will be someone who will help them, give them horses so they can ride to Wallingford, where her ally, Brien FitzCount, is waiting.

They are almost at the fires when a sentry on horseback comes towards them. They instantly stop, locked into position, heads bowed against their chests. They are wearing white bonnets and white nightgowns. The snow erases their bodies, but perhaps it doesn't completely erase their outlines, for the sentry halts before them. Matilda can hear the horse breathing, can hear it snort. The horse knows that they're there. She raises her head a little, can make out the upright figure of the man in the saddle. She sees him lift his arm, thinks he is going for his sword, but he blesses himself instead, blesses himself and rides right past them. He must have thought that they were ghosts.

In that moment when Matilda is standing perfectly still, trying to be invisible, she realizes that this is what she's learned from the three months in the castle. She's learned how to watch and wait. She's learned how to choose what burns, how much heat there will be in her maid's sewing box, in the wooden bowl that used to hold apples. She saw the river freeze, that moment when the water took hold of itself and wouldn't let go. All this time she thought the siege was chaos, but she can see now that it was really calm masquerading as chaos. If she gets away, the control she thinks she has in riding to Wallingford, in going back into battle against Stephen – that will prove to be the real chaos.

Matilda holds her breath. She lets it go. The horseman has passed and the knight in front of her has begun to move them, once more, across the frozen river. There is nothing to do but go forward.

1205

When Thomas goes into the storeroom behind the alehouse, he sees immediately that they are in trouble, rushes upstairs to wake his brother.

"Robert," he says, shaking the blanket-covered lump on the bed by the wall. "Robert, wake up. The ale has frozen solid."

It has been cold since Candlemas, and now, in the middle of February, the cold has just kept tightening its grip. It has moved deep inside every house, deep into the heart of every man.

Robert shucks his blanket in one angry movement. He cannot bear any more. There will never be a spring. He will never get warm. He sits on the edge of his bed, his head resting in his hands. A low moan escapes his lips.

Thomas is over by the small frost-encrusted window. "I suppose," he says, his back to his brother, "that if the mighty Thames can freeze over, then something as trifling as ale could freeze as well."

"We're ruined," says Robert, into the bowl of his hands. His breath snaps back at him, the only warmth there is in the room.

"I suppose," says Thomas, "if we slept with the jugs of ale, we might be able to keep them warm."

"We will perish," says Robert, but Thomas doesn't hear him, because he is still speaking into his hands, transfixed by the feeling of his own warm, used breath on his face.

"I doubt," says Thomas, "that anyone will hold us

to fault for such a thing. There has never been such a cold winter."

"Cold winter," says Robert, from the bed. "Freezing cold bloody awful winter."

Thomas turns from the window, his face lit up with his sudden good idea. "I think," he says, "there's profits to be made here."

At the mention of money, Robert perks up, lifts his head, and looks towards his younger brother. "How?" he says.

"When ale is frozen, it expands. We can't sell it as we used to, but we can   " Thomas pauses for effect, even though he doesn't need to, for Robert is listening intently. "We can start to sell it by weight instead of volume."

1269

—

The oxen don't want to cross the frozen river. They stand at the edge of the ice, swaying in their yoke, pawing at the ground. In front of them the frosted Thames seems as vast and wild as a moor, fog drifting like smoke across the white, uneven surface.

Oxen are wise and the driver trusts their instincts. He relies on his oxen to tell him when it will rain by their refusal to leave their stalls. He understands their attachment to one another, knows that if an ox is separated from its partner in yoke it will bellow and roar, be as upset as any human would be who was parted from their mate. That is why the driver has brought both oxen with him this morning, to the edge of the river, even though he only requires one ox to pull the cart. He is hoping that by bringing both, each will be a comfort to the other. But instead they seem to be doubly stubborn, doubly wary of what they are being required to do.

The freezing of the Thames has been an unexpected gift to the ox driver. He transports grain in his small cart, from his farm on one side of the river, to the miller on the other side. If he can cross on the ice, instead of by road and bridge, it saves him a half-day's journey.

The driver has had this pair of oxen for a long time, since they were born and he was a younger man. He can't even remember how long that might be. Each year seems much like those on either side of it. Only this year is different, and this year is different only because the Thames has frozen solid. In his entire lifetime he has never come upon such a thing as this before.

The oxen are brothers. They understand one another in a way the driver envies, although he would never say this to anyone.

So now, here they are, at the edge of the frozen river. The driver wants to cross the ice. The oxen want to stay on shore. The driver knows it will do no good to talk to the oxen, to scold them, to force them forwards with a lashing. This will just make them afraid and more certain that they were right in feeling they should not cross the river. This will mean that they will be inclined to balk in the middle of crossing, to stay put out of dread and nervousness. What the driver and the oxen both know is that if the oxen don't want to move, they don't have to, nothing can make them.

The driver respects his oxen. He walks with them over the fields every day. He is beside them and knows them. He spends more time with them than he does with any other living being. So he knows what he must do to convince them to come with him across the ice.

Oxen are magic creatures. The tiny, buzzing bird that makes the honey, the smallest bird there is, is born from the ox. If this tiny, yellow-and-black bird dies, the only thing that will revive it is for it to be covered with mud and placed under the living body of an ox.

The driver feels sometimes that he is the small, buzzing bird, that he has been born from the body of an ox. And so now he darts ahead, onto the ice at the edge of the river, just like that small bird darting off in search of the honey flowers. He runs forwards and back, the rind of ice and snow crisp beneath his boots. The ice does not have the hollow ring of cobblestones. It feels heavier, more substantial, like the thick mud of the fields. There's a muffled finality to his steps that must sound reassuring to the oxen, because, as the driver turns to face the opposite shore, he hears the slow, measured weight of them moving trustingly on the ice behind him.

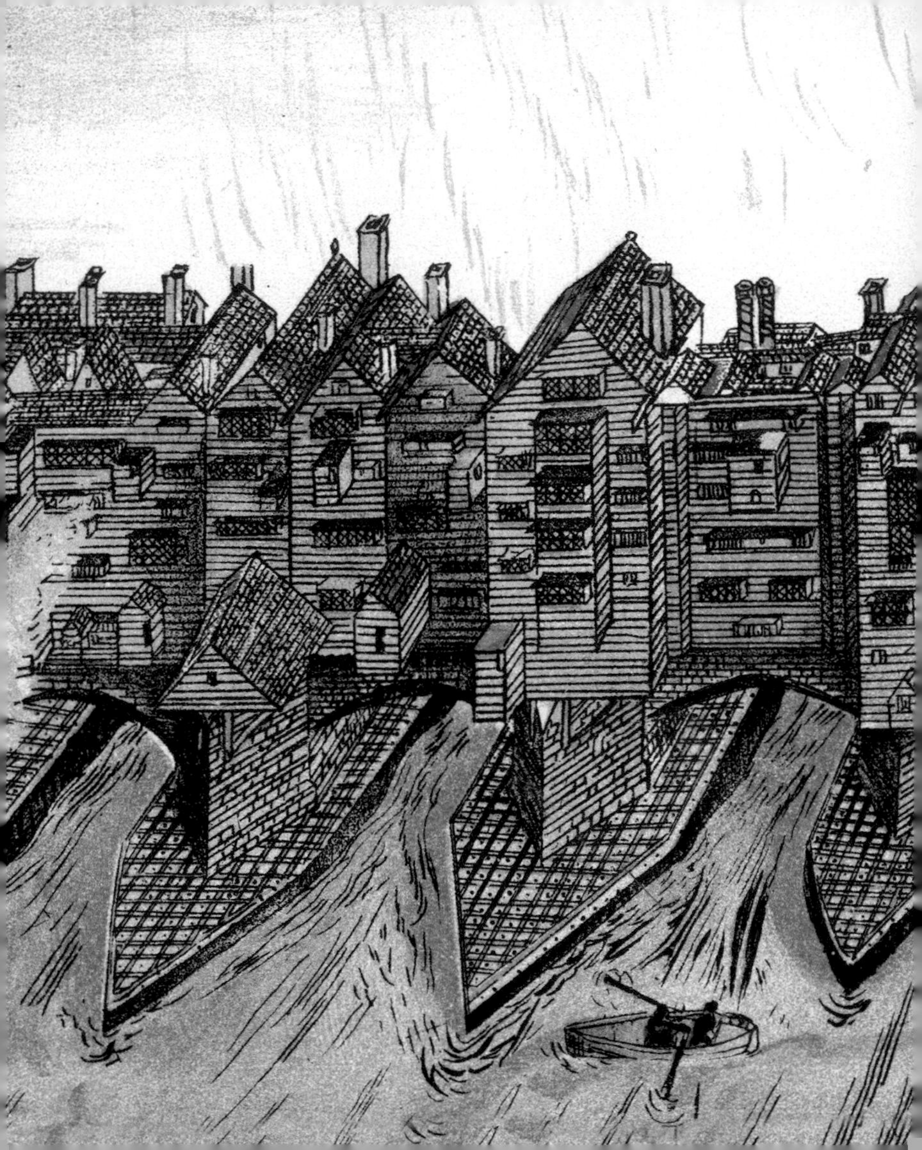

1282

—

I live atop the London Bridge, in a small stone house, on the fourth arch. I know this bridge, and I know the river below. I have seen all manner of weather. I know the swim of the tides and the rhythm of the boats that slip through the fast water under the arches. Each pier has a breakwater around it called a starling, and these starlings act like a dam, slow the water above the bridge, and squeeze it through the narrow chute of each arch into a fierce rapid. It is fine sport to shoot through these rapids in a small boat.

In the old times, the first times, the river was crossed using a ferry. It is said that when the last ferryman died, his daughter took all her wealth and used it to build a convent on a site that was thus named St. Mary of the Ovaries. The daughter's name, you see, was Mary Ovary. Later, priests made a school in the place of that convent. They were the ones who built the first of many wooden bridges across the river.

It was a priest who, much later, in 1176, designed and constructed this stone bridge upon which I live. It took thirty-three years to complete. There are gatehouses at either end and a church in the middle, St. Thomas's, named after Thomas Becket. There are nineteen arches, including one that has a draw-bridge that can be raised to allow the tall ships to enter the river below the bridge.

I have lived on this bridge for as long as I can remember, as long as I have been alive. Our house is newly built, for there was a fire on the bridge in 1212, just three years after the final work had been finished. The fire started on one side, and people rushed over from the other side to help quell the flames. But the wind was strong that day, and blew sparks across the bridge, catching the other end on fire, so that both ends were burning towards the middle, and the people on the bridge were trapped between advancing walls of flame.

Three thousand bodies were plucked from the water below, the dead choosing to jump rather than burn, and dying all the same.

I think of that fire when I lie in bed at night. I can almost hear the hiss and whisper of the flame as it slinks across the bridge towards me.

But it is not fire that comes. It is ice. This winter is the coldest I can remember. The river shuts tight below me. I can see the men and oxen walking across it as though it were a road. Sometimes I can even hear the groans of the river under the ice, a groan like a dying animal, or a sleeping man.

I am lucky to live on the fourth arch, because when the ice started to break up, it shouldered through the archways and crashed against the starlings, and five of the arches towards the middle of the bridge collapsed. Ice is stronger than water, that is what I have learned. Ice is made from water, but it does not seem to remember water.

Five arches collapsed and houses were pitched from the bridge. Walls crumbled and timbers snapped. The bridge survived the fire, but it does not look as though it will be able to survive the ice.

London Bridge is falling down. Falling down. Falling down.

London Bridge is falling down. My fair lady.

1309

—

The hare is set upon the ice. Here, it does not have the shelter of the field, cannot dash between furrow and stubble, use its colours to try to match the colours of the earth. Here, it is quick brown against this long, white river. There is nowhere for it to hide or escape. It will be run down by the dogs and torn to pieces.

This winter is so cold that loaves of bread will freeze unless wrapped in a layer of straw. The ice is so thick upon the river that it has damaged the starlings around the piers of the bridge. People have made a huge fire, there by the bridge, and even with the flames shooting higher than a man's head, there is no danger that the ice below will begin to melt.

I am the fewterer for this hare coursing. It is my task to lead the two greyhounds out onto the ice in leash, and to loose them when the hare has been given a bit of a lead. Behind me, behind the dogs, are the horsemen and footmen, the ones who have wagered on this race, the ones who own the hounds. Right now I am the most powerful person on this stretch of ice. I will be the one to set everything moving.

A hare will not run in a straight line. It will dodge and weave, moving in a criss-cross pattern over the ground. At first a greyhound will follow the exact positioning of the hare and, because the dog is a good deal larger and more ungainly than the hare, it will overshoot, will stumble, will have to double back, will fall behind. The better the dog, the sooner he will realize that he doesn't have to follow the hare so exactly, that he can anticipate the direction the hare might be heading, that he can run a straight line, gaining ground on the hare and cutting it off. The hare is locked into running the way he does. He cannot help himself, but the dog can. The dog is not such a bundle of nerves and instinct. The dog can think for himself, can work things out. The dog has all the advantages, and doesn't have to worry about its survival the way the hare does.

I do not think it is fair to bring what is meant for the field out onto the ice. The hare is too visible. The surface is too slick. There is nowhere for the hare to run, unless he can make it to shore. But to do this he must cross a vast, flat expanse of frozen river, and the dogs will almost certainly run him down when he gets to this part of the course.

There is a point for the lead dog at the first turn, a point for the dog that leads the hare, a point for the dog that turns the hare, and a point for the kill.

The hare was scooped from a field yesterday morning. It has been kept in a box covered with a horse blanket until now. It will be frightened and confused, will run as hard as it can to get away. I saw it shivering in its box before it was set loose. A large hare, all baggy skin, starving from this long, cold winter.

The dogs are the dogs of noblemen. They are well fed, kept indoors, treated with more kindness than most men. It is considered an act of murder to kill a greyhound. There is a law in place that states exactly that. It is murder and a man may be put to death for it, just as if he had killed another man.

The dogs are more important than I am. No one would care if I froze to death this winter, but the dogs will never be allowed to suffer as I've been suffering. The dogs will lie on velvet cushions by a blazing hearth. They will be fed from the tables of lords. Some say the dogs even sleep in bed with the noblemen.

The dogs are racing one another. The noblemen will ride up behind them and keep mind of their score. The dog who catches and kills the hare will undoubtedly be the victor.

A fewterer's job is to loose the hounds at a precise moment, the moment when the hare is just out of reach. It is a moment that is felt rather than measured.

I know it in my bones, and the dogs know it too, know when I have waited too long, strain against their leashes to tell me that I have waited too long to release them.

The thing about ice that I have noticed is that it is hard to judge the distance of a moving object upon it. In a field there are markers to gauge that movement. It is easy to see how fast the hare is running, how much ground it is covering, how far ahead it is. The big, empty whiteness of this frozen river makes all of that harder to judge. Only a man with a keen eye, a man who was used to the feeling of distance, or a dog who had run a coursing, would know that the hare has been allowed a longer run than it should have been allowed.

This is the most I can do without being caught and punished, without my small wage and the loaf of bread and bottle of ale I have been promised being kept from me. The hare has good instincts. He has started across the wide part of the river towards the far shore. I slip the leashes of the hounds and let them go.

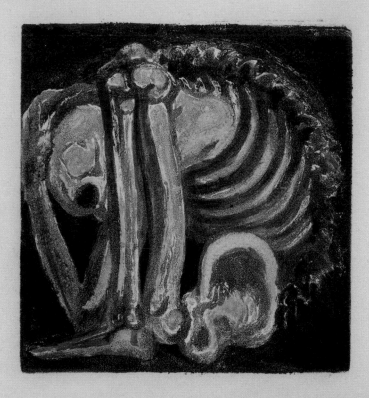

1363

I look for you along the banks of the river, where the great fires have been laid. Each fire a pyramid of coal, taller than the tallest man, and blazing with a fierceness that seems to match my need to find you.

You're not there, by any of the fires, nor at any of the tables that have been set upon the ice for this enormous feast. You promised you would come, and yet you haven't, and so I cannot settle, walk along one bank to the end of the coal fires, and then back along the other bank.

Here at Reading, the Thames has frozen so thickly that it will hold up the pyramids of burning coal without a quiver. It will hold up the long tables laden with food, at which sit all the poor and weak in the town. For one night only, for this night, we are to be treated to a great feast by the Abbot and the Grey Friar monks. The brothers themselves are acting in our service for the evening, fetching us food and drink when we so desire it.

I would be enjoying this, but I am too worried about whether or not you will arrive as promised. I know your family has been ill. You might have stayed to tend to them.

I am standing on the ice, a little way out from the fires so that I am not blinded by the flames, so that I can still see you if you come walking from the north end of the river. I am wearing a new black cloak I have fashioned from a blanket. It is not the green cloak you are used to seeing me in, and I worry that you will not recognize me, so I am determined to recognize you first. I don't like the new law that has been passed this year, decreeing that only the nobility are permitted to wear coloured clothing, and that each of the colours is coded with meaning. As the lower orders, we are only allowed black or grey. They can have red to signify their superior position, blue to show their fidelity, yellow to flash hostility, pale grey for sorrow, and green for love.

It seems an impossible law to enforce, and yet I have complied, and in my acceptance I show my fear of disobeying.

All around me, at all the tables set upon the frozen river, there is great merriment. The monks have provided each table with a hogshead of ale, and some of the merriment is caused by the generous taking of this ale.

And suddenly, there you are. You walk towards me over the ice, the fires throwing you into shadow, lighting you boldly with each surge and ebb of flame. You have recognized me, even in the new cloak. You walk towards me without hesitation, and my body feels suddenly weightless, as though I could float up like a bird, look down upon this little stretch of ice with the orange puddles of light bleeding at the edges, and the black lines of the tables laid out in the centre of the river.

When you are almost upon me, I move forward so that I may clasp you in my arms, but you hold out your hands to stop me. You, too, are wearing a black cloak, and there is frost decorating the ends of your hair where it touches your face. Not frost, I realize with a start, not frost but frozen tears.

"What?" I say, and my breath unknots in the cold night air, drifts off into threads of smoke.

You pull back the sleeve of your cloak and hold your bare arm out for me to see the black boils that are pockmarked over your flesh.

The Black Death.

It seemed as though the plague had passed. For more than ten years people died. Every second house in London seemed affected. There were so many dead that they were just tossed into massive pits, piled one on top of the other with no ceremony or marker. The nobility fled to the country, and then, when it all seemed to be over, they came back and passed this law about the clothes. This is to keep us in our place, because, with so many dead, the poor have become less so, have inherited money and property from those who have died.

You hold out your arm and I see the black spots, know that you probably already have the fever, that you will be dead in two or three days, and I cannot bear it.

All around us I can hear the sounds of people being happy – laughter and talking. I cannot remember this kind of happiness, not ever, and it seems so wrong that a moment so good could lie peacefully alongside a moment so bad.

If I touch you, I will be infected. You probably shouldn't have come here, because you now carry the disease, and because it has most likely taken all your strength just to get here. But I am glad you kept your promise, and I am more than glad to see you. I don't know how I can live without you, or if I will. It was only days ago that I last saw you, that I touched you.

The plague could be bubbling under my skin as we stand here.

I lift my cloak so that you can see the lining, so that you can see what I've wanted to tell you. I have sewn pieces of my green cloak into the lining of this black one. Green for love, under the new law.

It seems strange that this is the end of the world, this scene of feasting and happiness, something that is so outside my usual days. But perhaps that is good, perhaps if I had to leave a world that was my own it would be harder.

You lower your arm and smile. You have understood. I step forward into your embrace and kiss you.

1408

The birds fall from the trees. They tumble from the roofs and chimney-pots where they have perched. They are heavier in death than they were in life. Solid and flightless, they fall to the ground like dark, feathered apples, with exactly that weight, the weight of an apple.

There has been a frost for fourteen weeks straight and everything is starving. The Thames has frozen solid. The fires burn so fiercely in the hearths of the houses that sometimes the houses themselves catch into flame, a bright bloom of red flaring up in the field of white that is now London.

Everyone, everything, is starving, but it is the birds that are dying. They die fast and the songbirds go first, all the delicate notes of the thrushes and blackbirds stopped in their throats. They drop from the trees, songless. They fall from the railings of the bridge onto the frozen river below. At the threshold of every house, the hinge of every gate, the surface of every road, lie the small, cold bundles of bird.

A woman walks on the ice below London Bridge. She is hunched against the weather, keeping her head down to avoid the wind that whistles between the stone arches of the bridge. A bird falls at her feet. Another hits her shoulder and bounces off her body onto the river.

The woman goes home and tells her husband: "I was hit by a bird that fell from the sky." And later on – the next morning, or the morning after that – she will be dressing herself for the day and will see the bruise that has flowered on her shoulder. A bruise as dark and rich as the colour of a blackbird's wing.

1434

It is almost the same distance by road as by river from Gravesend to London, but it is a completely different journey. Moving the wine by barge was a peaceful, slow drift up the Thames. It was fishermen and green fields and cows drinking at the water's edge, lifting their heads to watch the boat sail by.

Now that the whole length of the river has frozen, all the way from London Bridge to Gravesend, John must make the journey overland. The wine has been loaded onto a cart, and the driver seems determined to take them over the roughest roads he can find. The wheels of the cart groan and squeak, clatter against the hard, rutted earth. The jugs of frozen wine knock together like stones. The horses shift in their creaking harness, and the driver whistles a low, tuneless whistle all the way, except for when he tries to engage John in mindless chatter about the pain in his legs. The noise is all too much, and once John has delivered the wine to the merchants and made it home, at the end of a very long day, he is in a foul temper.

"I can't abide any more tumult," he says, striding into his house and slamming the door so hard that the dog begins to bark and wakes the baby.

Annabelle looks up at him blankly. She has been sitting quietly by the fire with the middle boy on her lap. The dog had been lying at her feet. The baby had been sleeping.

John kicks the dog and lumbers towards the warmth of the hearth, collapsing into a chair with a long, dramatic groan. He pulls a jug of frozen wine out from the inside pocket of his coat and sets it in front of the fire.

"All of it bloody frozen," he says.

Annabelle continues to regard him blankly, and it occurs to John that her name, which she's proud to consider as French, is really the name of a cow.

The winter has been long and harsh and very cold. The small house they live in has only one fireplace, this one, downstairs, and so, over the course of the winter, everything has migrated towards the hearth. Chairs are pushed right up to the grate. The table is spitting distance from the fire. Clothes are hung above it and boots are warmed before it. All the beds have been moved downstairs and are arranged in an arc around the flickering coal. No one has been upstairs in weeks. The last time John climbed the stairs to the attic it was so frigid up there that he might as well have been scaling the tallest mountain peak.

"I'm hungry," he says. He has been gone two full days, living on bread and cheese and beer, which at the time seemed well enough, but now seems to have been a great and painful deprivation.

"Supper's in the pot," says Annabelle, but she makes no move to disturb the sleeping child in her lap and fetch the food for her husband.

"Well," says John, hurt that she has refused to serve him. "I'm hungry, but I'll wait for the wine." He glares at the jug by his feet, nudges it a little closer to the fire with his toe. It still seems completely frozen, although the outside of the jug has started to bead with water.

"Suit yourself," says Annabelle. She shifts the boy on her knee, and he whimpers in his sleep like a dog.

"We are living in the fireplace," says John, looking around at the cluster of furniture huddled up against the hearth. "It is not proper for a man to have to live in the fireplace."

36

Annabelle says nothing. The dog, with a wary glance at John, slinks back towards the fire and settles down on a scrap of rug by Annabelle's feet.

John stares at the jug of wine, willing it to melt. The freezing of the Thames has changed everything for him. All that once allowed him, included him, has now locked him out. Once, he moved up the slow water of the river, moved in the soft embrace of his wife. Once, the sweet relief of wine released his good humour, flushed him warm, full of happiness.

"It's cold out here," he says, but no one hears him.

1506

——

The three boys have come down to skate on the river. The water above the bridge has set fast and smooth. There is no snow on the surface and the ice glistens black under the winter sun. It is early in the morning and there is no one else moving on the Thames.

The boys sit on the ice at the edge of the shore and strap the skate bones onto their boot soles. They push off from the bank, at first tentatively, and then with stronger and stronger strokes, until they are flying, like crooked birds, up the centre of the river.

At first Samuel thinks he is just heating up from the exercise, from the effort of pushing his body across the ice. But the sweat starts to run from his face like rain. His hair is wet and plastered to his head, and he can feel, by their heaviness, that his clothes are soaked. He stops. His legs feel shaky, uncertain about holding him upright. His friends are now far ahead of him, swooping and gliding up the river, moving fast and far away from him.

It is most surely the *swetynge sykenesse*, and the thought of this makes Samuel wobble and crash to the ice.

The *swetynge sykenesse* has suddenly come back this year after many years of being absent. This second outbreak is not as virulent as the first, but people are still dropping dead in terrifying number.

The sickness kills swiftly and without warning. There is a sudden, burning sweat, and then a fever, and the person thus afflicted could be dead within the hour. It kills people as it finds them – sleeping in their beds, gathering firewood on the heath, walking to market. Unlike the Black Death, it seems to be a peculiarly English disease. There has been no word of it affecting the French.

Samuel is now too weak to cry out, to call loud enough for his friends to hear him. He curls up on the ice, presses his cheek against the surface. The cold feels good, but soon the ice beneath his cheek turns to water. He is burning a hole through to the river below, and he imagines falling into that water and floating there amongst the fishes. He closes his eyes. He can hear the fish swimming, the scrape of their fins moving through the water. They brush against him and lift him up, drag him along the bottom of the river.

Samuel opens his eyes. His friends have him by the arms, one on one side of his body, one on the other. They are lifting him and pulling him. He can hear their laboured breathing. He can see the ice spray up from their skates.

But he still feels like a fish, swimming in his own sweat, gasping for air. They have hooked him, caught him, are reeling him in. He starts twitching, trying to wriggle free of their grasp. If they get him to shore, they will kill him. They will split his head upon a rock and run a knife along his belly. They will sink their plundering hands deep into his flesh and haul out his steaming entrails. His only hope is to shake them off, here in the water, where he can still get away, where he can still save his life.

1515

He has walked the frozen river every day, all this long, cold winter. He doesn't walk to watch the skaters on the ice, or the carts and oxen crossing from one side to the other with their loads of grain or apples. He doesn't look at the sky, empty now of birds, or up at the arches of the bridge, each one gaping open like a hungry mouth. None of these things is as interesting to this man as the river itself. He walks along, only looking down at the ice in front of his boots.

He is an explorer. Well, not quite an explorer yet, but he wants to become one. All this year and last year there has been talk of a passage through the polar ice at the top of the world, and he has listened to all of this speculation and pondered upon it. Several attempts have been made to find the way, but all have ended before they reached the polar seas. This man wants to be on the next ship that leaves England for such a purpose.

And so he is studying the properties of ice in order to prepare himself for the vast stretches of it that await him in the Northwest Passage. Every day he treks along the Thames as though he were walking in the Arctic wastes. He keeps his eyes down to observe the ice, and so he won't have to see any other people, the chimneys of the houses on the banks, so he can imagine that he is the only living, moving creature in an endless white landscape.

He has made a vow to himself to keep walking on the ice until he falls through it and he intends to keep this vow. It makes him feel that what he is doing is dangerous, and he needs that feeling of danger to keep the image of himself as an explorer alive.

At the beginning of the freeze, the beginning of winter, the ice is clear and dark, like tar. As it melts it softens, the whole sheet of it sagging the way a floor does from having weight on it in the same place year after year.

Snow shows the veins of brown leaves on the surface. The leaves have collapsed on the gravelly rind, their tracery fine as lace.

When the sun's warmth dissolves the snow into the ice, it becomes milky as the body of a fish. The leaves and sticks that have frozen into it filter light and heat through their skins, make themselves into islands, rings of water form around them, and they eventually burn themselves through to the water below.

The ice seems to melt from above and below at the same time. Holes appear at random, and water pools on the surface. Each section of ice seems to be different from the one next to it.

When the explorer finally does fall through the ice, it is swift and sudden, not the gentle lowering he had expected. He scrapes his shins on the jagged edges of the hole on the way down and then, because he has plunged through quite close to shore and the water is shallow, he climbs out awkwardly and walks home, the cold river water stiffening the hinges of his body shut.

At home, drying by the fire, drinking hot milk, the explorer wonders at the wisdom of what he has been doing. He has been trying to learn the properties of ice, but all he has learned is that ice is diverse, that no piece of ice matches another. He has wanted to learn the ice in preparation for walking on the empty Arctic plains, but what he has perhaps done instead is learn the frozen Thames.

1536

I have waited by the side of the river for ages now, hoping to get a glimpse of the King. We were told yesterday that he would be travelling down from Greenwich today, but no one is certain when this might be. There is a small group of us gathered at the bend of the Limehouse Reach, waiting for the royal carriage to pass us on its way to London. It's not that I can afford such an idle morning as this, but I also cannot pass up the spectacle of a coach and four being driven down the middle of the frozen Thames. I might never see such a sight again in my life.

It is said that the King performed such a feat mere days ago, but I missed seeing that passage. The river has been frozen a while now, and I am used to the skaters and the carts and the people walking about on the ice. But to see the King in his royal carriage use the river as a highway – that is a different matter altogether.

It is also mere days ago that the King's first wife, Catherine of Aragon, died, and I wonder if somehow the events are related – if the journey down the frozen river has not a little to do with the death of a woman King Henry once loved. She died in Kimbolton Castle, in Huntingdonshire, where she had been confined, and perhaps she died of the winter, as so many have this year. Perhaps the castle was draughty and cold and she perished because of that.

It is cold where I stand. I have to keep stamping my feet like a horse to keep the blood flowing to them. My breath hangs in a foggy sack and hardens into ice crystals on my muffler. I'm not sure how

much longer I'll be able to wait here without freezing to death myself.

The rumours about the King, of which there are
always many, whisper that he might be tiring of the
woman he divorced Catherine of Aragon for – Anne
Boleyn – and that he is gathering evidence against
her so that she may be charged with adultery. If this
proves to be true, and the charges go forward, she
would most certainly be put to death by hanging.
Adultery is a treasonous offence.

I was more partial to the old Queen than I am to
the new one, but still I feel sympathy for Anne
Boleyn, and for Princess Elizabeth, her daughter,
who is not yet three years old. A motherless child is
something to be pitied.

There's a cheer gone up farther along the bank,
and I hear the coach and four before I see it – hear
the rumbling of the horses' hooves on the ice, deeper
than the clatter on cobblestones. Each hoof-beat
sounding like a muffled bell in the cold morning air.

The horses are white and the coachman is dressed
in scarlet and inside the carriage, out of our sight, is

the grieving or plotting King of England.

We stand on the bank and wave and cheer, regardless of whether our King is full of sorrow or full of rage. It matters not this morning. What matters is that the horses are as white as the snow, that they look both magnificent and ghostly as they pass, and that the sound of the hooves and the carriage is deep as a bell, deep as our own heartbeats sunken in our chests. What matters is that we have waited for this. We have waited for this, and it has come to us.

1565

The Queen shoots at prickes set upon the ice. She has done this every morning since the river froze. I have been her companion in this pursuit, guiding her onto the Thames, placing the targets out for her, assisting with the longbow and arrows.

At first the Queen took many men out on the river with her. There was a man to carry the bow, another to secure the prickes to the ice, a few to guard her royal presence, one who carried a chair in case she might want to rest from her exertions. At first, perhaps, the Queen did not know what to expect from the ice. She acted as though it were the same as a journey out to the palace fields. She took the same number of men as she would have taken with her on those occasions.

But the ice is not the same as the earth. To step out from the banks, to view the palace and the grounds from the solid surface of the river, that is something that happens but once in a lifetime, and one need not behave the same on the ice as one does on land.

After the third morning the Queen understood this. She bade the others stay behind and took only me, her chambermaid, with her. On the fourth morning she bade me dress as a boy, a page, so that it might be easier for me to accomplish my tasks without the burden of the long dresses I usually wear.

The ice is quiet and demands the same. That is why the Queen likes to journey out onto it in the mornings with only me as company, because it is the closest she ever gets to being alone. The ice is like a whisper, constantly shushing us into its silence.

Since it has come to be only the Queen and myself on the frozen river, the men must go out earlier than we to place the prickes upon the ice. Each pricke is the mark of a compass painted onto wood and fitted into a stand. The men do not put the targets in the same place each time. Perhaps they forget where they were the previous morning, and all the ice looks similar enough to them that they cannot distinguish between one place and another. I like it that we have to hunt the targets down each day, as though they are real prey and we are actually in the hunting fields.

I walk behind the Queen, carrying the longbow and the quiver of arrows. I like the feeling of freedom I have wearing leggings, how much lighter I seem, how much movement is possible. We have been together long enough, the Queen and I, that we need say very little to one another, and I like that too. There's no need to explain or question. I know what is required of me and I have learned Her Highness well enough by now to predict what she will do in any given situation.

But the ice is new to us. The old ways of behaving

LONDINVM FERACISSIMI AN-
GLIAE REGNI METROPOLIS

don't seem to apply here, and in the absence of new ways we hang in a quiet and cautious place. It is as though, in the very fact that the river froze, anything else might suddenly become possible as well.

There is certainly change about these days. Captain Hawkins returned from the New World with potatoes and tobacco, and much talk has taken place at the palace lately as to the merits of each. The potato is regarded suspiciously as being a sort of poison weed, but tobacco is being embraced as a substance of wonder and amazement. It is thought to be one of the best things yet brought home from the New World, and Captain Hawkins has been much praised for his discovery.

The prickes are not set too far out this morning, and we find them quite easily. I lay the bow and arrows on the ice and reach up behind the Queen to remove her robe. She extends her left arm without a word, and I lace on the leather close-sleeve to protect her forearm from the snap of the bow string. She lowers her left arm and extends her right, and I button on her shooting glove.

A longbow should be the height of the person who uses it. It should be as their shadow. The Queen's bow is made from the supplest ash and her arrows are fitted with only the prized feathers of the grey goose. She is a good shooter and enjoys it, can handle a longbow or crossbow as well as any man, and yet I know that this shooting on the ice is not so much about the shooting as it is about the ice. The shooting is the reason to be out here, but it is the river itself that calls us back every day.

The Queen takes up the bow and fits it with an arrow. I stand a little to the side and behind her, holding her robe over my arm. The sun is out and quivering in the sky above us. The ice of the river sparkles and the red hair of my Queen sparkles and the arrow flies fast and true to its mark. My body is warm and the world is cold and I feel, not like a maid, or a page, but like myself, and I do not know what to call this if not happiness.

1608

—

By all accounts, Bess of Hardwick is a lucky woman. She is one of the wealthiest women in Britain, second only to the Queen. Each of her four marriages has increased her wealth considerably. She has six living children. She has built and owned some of the finest homes in England – Chatsworth, Oldcoates, Hardwick Hall. In 1601, she even undertook an inventory of all her possessions, had pages and pages written up with a list of items such as *a stoole of cloth of golde tyssued and black*

tuftaffetie and an Iron for seacole, a payre of tonges.
Even though her fourth marriage has ended badly, and her husband, the Earl of Shrewsbury, has called her, strangely enough, a "sharp, bitter shrew," Bess is largely satisfied with her rather generous portion of life's banquet.

But Bess has a secret. She has told it to no one. She believes it to be true.

It is those things we believe in that prove to be our undoing. Believe in love and you will be forsaken. Believe in your own good health and you will be sorely afflicted.

Bess believes that if she stops building she will be struck dead. She has been told as much by her trusted fortune teller. She believes in the words of her fortune teller, goes to visit her in London to hear of all the good things that will soon befall her. She wasn't expecting these words of dire prediction.

It is not difficult for Bess to keep building. She loves to build. Her latest triumph, Hardwick Hall, has earned her the title Bess of Hardwick. It is a magnificent structure, four storeys tall, each storey higher than the one below it. There are so many windows in the building that it has inspired the rhyme *Hardwick Hall – more glass than wall*. She is so proud of this building that she has had her initials – E.S. – carved in stone letters at the head of the towers. Begun in 1590, there is still work to be done on the hall, so it is not a matter of there not being anything to build. The problem isn't the lack of work. The problem is the weather.

Last year, all was water. This year, everything is ice.

Last winter a huge wave struck the coast of Bristol. Cardiff was also badly affected and the water swept fourteen miles inland. The dead were washed out of the graveyards, and the water climbed so high that it left lines on the walls of the surviving church-es taller than any man. The hills of water were so fast and strong that no greyhound could have raced swifter to its prey. Two thousand people died, and it was written in a pamphlet Bess saw in London on one of her visits to the fortune teller that the wave was as though *the greatest mountains in the world had ouer-whelmed the lowe valeyes.*

This winter the Thames has frozen. Crowds gather upon it, booths have been set up to sell ale and food. There is bowling and dancing. A shoemaker has established shop, and a barber cuts hair. It is said that if you have your hair cut on the frozen river it is something you will remember in the afterlife.

The river is frozen and so everything also freezes. Puddles are small icy windows laid upon the earth. You can travel a hundred miles and not see a thrush or blackbird. Mortar freezes before it can be spread.

Bess has had her workmen mix the mortar with hot ale in an effort to make it stick, but this has been to no avail. If the mortar won't stick to the bricks, then she cannot continue to build and all that the fortune teller warned her about will come to pass.

Perhaps it has already come to pass, for Bess has been ill with a fever for a few weeks now. She lives in her chamber with her maid in constant attendance, and even though she is an old woman of eighty, she is not ready to die and she fears it.

Outside the wind howls and the weather continues cold and icy. The Thames stays frozen. Each day

Bess sends word for the workmen to try mixing the mortar with hot ale again, and each day she is sent word back that this hasn't been successful.

Bess is dying and she knows it. She believes in the words of her fortune teller, but really, anyone could have told her that if you have to stop doing the thing you love, it will kill you.

1621

—

"Mullet," says Henry.

He is peering down at the space between his boots where, just visible below the surface, there is a sizable fish, frozen into the ice.

"It's not grey," says William. He is down on his hands and knees, face right up against the river. "Carp. It might be carp."

"Not big enough."

"Gudgeon."

"Flounder."

"Flounder!" William raises his head, incredulous at his friend's idiocy. "When was the last time you were after catching a flounder in the Thames?"

"Could be," says Henry. "Could be a flounder."

"Because you want it to be so, then it must be?"

"No," says Henry, lying.

"Bullhead," says William.

"It's not a bullhead."

"Not the fish. You."

The men are silent for a moment. All around them is the swirling noise of the Frost Fair, booths set upon the ice with all manner of goods for sale. Out towards the centre of the river, men are skating. They have fastened the leg bones of sheep onto the soles of their boots, and push themselves along with wooden staffs that have been shod with iron. Sometimes their velocity overtakes their competence and the skaters run into one another, often with poles upraised, risking death by impalement.

"Remember when there was too much fish?" says William.

Once, British noblemen fed so much salmon to their servants that the servants had a revolt and there was a law passed to limit salmon rations to a mere three times a week.

Now, with the Thames in this frozen state, there is not enough fish. The fishmongers have gone out of business and the butchers are thriving, taking their custom.

Henry regards the fish between his boots. It is held fast in the act of swimming, shadowy with the murk of the river surrounding it. He supposes they might be able to chip it out of the ice, but it seems a long way down and the effort involved would be too great. He wonders what it was like for the fish to freeze like that, whether it felt it, body slowing, stiffening up. How strange for water to suddenly become rock, for what was made of movement to be stopped.

"I suppose we all must die," he says, for it has just occurred to him that the fish is not only frozen, but dead.

William looks up. "What are you going on about?"

"Nothing."

There's the smack of two skaters colliding on the ice just beyond them. One of the men is lying on the river now, rolling about and moaning and holding on to his leg.

"Tench," says William, his attention already turning away from the injured man and back to the frozen fish.

Henry is seized with a fear of dying. He doesn't want to slow and stiffen, turn to rock. He doesn't want to exist in a frozen state until the end of time. It doesn't seem right that it could happen to him. It all seems alarmingly unfair.

"Well?" says William.

"Loach," says Henry. "Stone Loach."

1635

—

The fourteen men assemble on the ice and, without speaking, divide themselves into two teams. Even in the midst of winter the sun is strong and they soon shed their coats and gloves, run down the frozen river in their shirt-sleeves, shunting the football before them.

It is Sunday morning. They should be in church, but they have come instead to the river to play football. They feel no guilt for their decision. It is glorious to be young and in motion, to be hurtling down the icy pitch towards the opposite goal with no thoughts in their heads other than those of winning the game. Church would have been a waste of such a day. Church would have meant sitting still, denying the urgency of their living bodies to move, to revel in the pleasures of the flesh.

The game is not long begun when the two teams of boys come together in a scrum, a little way out from the bank of the river. Perhaps it is the strength of the sun, or the fact that the ice has been set a long time and is weakening. Perhaps it is because all fourteen boys in one spot is too much for the ice to bear. Or perhaps it is something else – the Lord making judgment on their sin for using His day to serve themselves.

What happens next is that the ice gives way and the boys plunge into the cold river water. They fall in together, arms and legs tangled into a knot of flesh. There are some who cannot swim, and some who cannot climb out from under the bodies of their friends. In all, eight of the lads perish, consigned for eternity to a cold, watery grave.

The vicar lays down his pen. He is not sure how to end his *Divine Tragedie*. He does not want to belabour the point that the drownings occurred because the boys were partaking of sport on the Sabbath, but he is afraid that if he just leaves it to his readers they might blame the ice instead of respecting the wrath of the Lord. Probably he has given them too many choices. Perhaps it is best not to mention the strength of the sun or the age of the ice.

The vicar hugs himself. It is so cold in the vestry that he can see his breath. It has not been difficult to imagine the boys flailing about in the icy river water.

None of this really happened. It is a tale invented by the vicar so that his congregation will remain God-fearing, will not be tempted by the wondrous occurrence of the Thames freezing over and forget their duty to the Lord. God must maintain supremacy over all earthly delights, even those that seem miraculous themselves.

The vicar rubs his nose. The tip is completely frozen. He cannot feel his own pinch.

He has been vigilant. He has not permitted

himself to visit the river at all, not even to catch a glimpse of it from the bell-tower. The booths erected upon it are for commerce, and the pursuits enjoyed on the ice are base and sinful. It would be entirely wrong for him to set foot in such a place.

But the vicar has imagined the ice, has seen the long, white stretch of it in his mind, can imagine the feeling of walking upon water.

He shakes his head. This isn't doing him any good at all. He might as well name what needs to be named, so that there is no mistaking the lesson.

He picks up his pen and begins to write.

Their deaths were a judgment sent down from almighty God. This judgment could have been avoided. We must not forget we are in service to the Lord. We are not free men.

1649

—

We placed the body of the King in the boat. The head was meant to decorate the spikes of Traitor's Gate, but Cromwell had relented and placed it in the boat as well, so that it could be sewn back onto the body in Windsor and the family could bury the man entire.

The head had been held up by the hair before the crowd and then the people had been let up to the block and, after paying, had been allowed to dip their handkerchiefs into the blood. The blood of a king will close any wound that it is brushed upon, will cure any illness that afflicts you.

The King wanted the block to be set higher, but it would go no higher. He gave the signal for his own execution by stretching out his arms. One stroke of the axe and it was over. He had said some last words, but no one could hear what they were. We did hear him ask the executioner if his hair was well. He wore a black cloak, took it off to be just in his waistcoat, and then put it on again for the execution.

We had not trusted that he would lay his head so obligingly upon the block. We had prepared hooks and staples with which to drag him to his slaughter if he had been unwilling. We did not trust that he would be anything other than arrogant, as he had been all through the trial. Even as the judgment was being read, the King would not admit to, or recognize, any of his faults.

The judgment was simply put: "He, the said Charles Stuart, as a truant, traitor, murderer and public enemy to the good of this nation, shall be put to death by severing of his head from his body."

It was difficult to try the King. I will admit that Cromwell fixed the vote to please himself and his ends. There were meant to be 135 judges, but only 68 showed up at the trial, and Cromwell let only 46 of these into the hall.

Charles was a tyrant who ruled only according to his will. He had governed England for eleven years without once calling parliament into session, and yet he seemed surprised when the people rose up against him. I almost admired him for this. I almost felt sorry for him.

It is cold today, the day we executed Charles I. It is a Tuesday, a cold Tuesday, the thirtieth of January. The King had a last meal this morning of bread and wine and, before that, he was permitted to walk his dog for a final time in St. James's Park. And now he is making the familiar journey from London to Windsor, but his coffin lies in this boat and the water of the Thames is in a frozen state. We have had to start south of the bridge, pole off the ice floes that surround the craft. It is a slow and difficult manoeuvre down the river.

To kill one's King is a solemn business. Even though many wanted him dead, I can attest that there was not a man who was not saddened by the sight of the sovereign's head upon the block. We need to believe in the power and justness of the Crown, and when that is thrown into question, so too is every-thing else and we are as we are – sailing down a frozen river with a headless man at the helm.

1655

I see it as I'm making my way home from the synagogue.

The synagogue is not really a synagogue. It's the rear of Abraham's house. It's actually a shed attached onto the rear of Abraham's house. We meet there in secret, the handful of Jews who live in this part of London and know of one another. We live not as Jews, but disguised as Spaniards because Jews have not been allowed to live in England since 1290.

In 1290, there was no tolerance for any religion except Catholicism and all Jews were expelled by Edward I.

But the times are better than they were. Catholicism is not the official religion any more, and some of us have made our way back and stayed, in secret. Cromwell has allowed religious freedom even as he has, strangely, banned theatre. But this does not mean that we can stop posing as Spaniards, can stop meeting in the shed at the rear of Abraham's house. Religious freedom does not extend to Judaism. But there is hope. Last year the Rabbi Manasseh, who lives in Amsterdam, sent his son, Samuel, to England to lobby Cromwell for re-admission. It is said that Cromwell is not opposed to consider such a request and, this year, the Rabbi himself intends to come and plead for the Jews to be allowed back into England.

I cannot imagine what it would feel like to walk down the street as myself, after all this time as Pedro Alvarez. I cannot pretend to know what it would feel like to walk to the synagogue with my friends, instead of arriving alone at Abraham's, slipping in under darkness, afraid of being discovered at the sin of worshipping in my own faith.

This is what I am thinking when I see the ship. I have been keeping my head bowed, out of habit, so that no one will look too long upon my face and recognize me for a Jew. I have been keeping my head bowed because it is night and dark out and I am travelling home without the aid of a light.

I imagine being free of my disguise, being able to return to myself, and I look up as I come around the corner of the street and I see it there, under the moon, silhouetted against the quay. It is an enormous ship, a web of rigging, a bowsprit the width of an ancient tree. It is an enormous ship and it is completely frozen into the ice. The ice has caught it, has pushed up against the hull and staved it in, snapped the massive timbers with ease. I can see the jagged mess that has been made of the hull, can see the strips of broken planks hanging from the side of the ship, the way hide hangs in flayed tatters from the side of a butchered ox.

It stops me. I stand there, by the edge of the river, and I cannot seem to walk any farther.

The ship was made for one thing and encountered another. Water is not recognizable as ice. But perhaps, even with the hole in its side, the ship will still float when the ice releases it. This is what I want – release. I can feel the tight grip of the ice around me, around my life, and what I want, this evening by the edge of the river, is to be cast back upon the water, to be set free.

1662

I have cleared my desk and swept the room. I have stood by the window one last time, by the altar one last time. I have knelt on the cold stone floor in the nave and I have risen without comfort.

It is a cold walk from the church and, since I am in no hurry, I take the path by the river so as to watch the skaters on the ice. It is on the frozen river this year that the new iron *scheets* from Holland are being used. They are far superior for sliding on the ice than the old skates made from animal bones. It is a marvel to see the swiftness with which the skaters move over the Thames, and I never tire of this sight.

It is strange to think that I have left the Church for good, that I will not be returning on Sunday to deliver my sermon, as usual; that I will not be spending Saturday hunched over my desk, blowing on my hands to keep them warm while I struggle to write that sermon. I used to write about many wondrous things, of beasts and distant lands, even of this frozen river. I cannot reconcile myself to the Act of Uniformity that is to be passed this year by parliament, and which states that the new Book of Common Prayer is to be used for all prayers and sacraments, and that it is to be the only text allowed in religious services. If this wasn't offence enough, now all priests must be ordained by Episcopal rule, as was the case years ago. We are to be servants of the Church of England, instead of being servants to God.

Charles II wants to abolish the religious freedoms that were granted during Cromwell's stay in power, and yet Charles is engaged to be married to Catherine of Braganza, the daughter of King John IV of Portugal. She is a Roman Catholic and will never be crowned Queen because Catholics are forbidden, under the new rules, to take part in Anglican services. The whole thing is ludicrous. I have spent my entire life in service to God, to my idea of God. What am I meant to do with my life now? I am good for very little else.

The river is busy today, full of revellers. I stand on the bank to watch the skaters. They glide effortlessly past me and I can hear the notching of their iron blades upon the surface of the ice. They pass alone, hands clasped behind their backs for balance. They pass in groups of two or three, holding on to one another's hands. I like their wordless flight along the river. If I were still employed by the Church, this is what I would choose to write my sermon on for Sunday's service. I would write about the frozen Thames, and the look of the skaters upon it, how the body well used is a celebration of the Glory of God.

The skaters on the ice appear to have no worries,

but I know this is not true. Each man and woman carries a burden that is sometimes impossible to bear. This year is particularly hard because the Hearth Tax has been introduced. The occupiers of each dwelling must pay two shillings for each hearth they possess. It hardly seems fair that, during one of the coldest winters in England, people must pay for their small portion of warmth.

The Hearth Tax. The rule of the Bishops once again. It is perhaps the same thing. Our liberties are being taken from us, and we are meant to pay for the things that we need in order to remain alive.

But there are the skaters. They have gone upriver and are now swooping back down towards me. They soar like birds, like I have always imagined the spirit soars when it is in the presence of the Lord. They move like they have no burdens, no worries, as if their lives do not cost them their lives.

1666

—

While I have been imprisoned in the house, much has happened. The people living in the house next to ours have died and the house has been pulled apart, used to feed the fires that burn up and down the street. The weather has grown colder and the Thames has frozen over, frozen solid. The great Irish healer, Valentine Greatrakes, has come to England.

And some things have not changed. The King and

the merchants, the lawyers, the clergy, and the doctors, are all still in the country. They fled there almost a year ago, at the first sign of the plague, and perhaps they will never return to London.

It was not easy to escape from the house. My father had the ring of red sores that begin the Black Death, and so we were all of us locked up in our house. A red cross was painted on the door to show our quarantine and a guard was posted so we could not leave. We were meant to be there for forty days and forty nights. In that time all who were infected would have died, although the others might also have died, as it was hard to get bribes out so that food could be brought in.

It was my brother's idea to kill the guard. *Why should we have to die?* he said. *When it is only father who is ill.*

We used a rope and fastened a noose on the end of it and lowered it from the attic window in the early dark of evening. My brother insisted that I lower the noose because, as a girl, I had a more delicate touch than he did. He has clumsy hands, is always doing things too roughly. The dog used to yelp when he tried to pet her. My brother has the falling sickness, would collapse suddenly into fits that were alarming to behold and then, as suddenly as they had come upon him, they would be over.

We lowered the noose from the attic window and snared the guard with it. Killing him was easier than I had imagined. He died with only a small flailing at the end of the rope. There did not seem to be much life in him to extinguish.

My mother would not leave my father, and so we left them. The world that we walked out to was cold and beautiful. Once we were past the plague fires and down by the river it was quieter too. It was strange not to see animals about. Even in the bustle of London there have always been cats and dogs. But the songbirds have perished in the cold winter, and the King has ordered all the dogs and cats within the city to be destroyed, as he fears that they are responsible for carrying the plague.

After such a long, hot summer, it is odd to come out into such a cold winter. We walked along the river in silence, grateful just to be walking, just to be outside again.

I am taking my brother to see The Stroker. That is the name that has been given to Valentine Greatrakes because he has the habit of stroking his hands over the part of the body that is afflicted. His hands can cure. His hands are the opposite of my brother's clumsy hands.

Valentine Greatrakes is in Whitechapel and we have heard, through one of the nurses that came to tend my father in our quarantine, that he will see anyone who visits him there. He has cured a woman with a thickness of hearing and helped a man with a lame leg to walk again. *The pain moves out slowly*, said the nurse. *Pain likes to stay and will not leave of a sudden.*

If the pain is in the shoulder, Valentine Greatrakes will stroke the shoulder and the pain will move to the elbow, then to the wrist, then to the hands, and finally, will travel out the tips of the fingers. *People feel it as a great coldness leaving their bodies*, said the nurse.

My father will die. Perhaps my mother will also die, tending him so closely in that house with the red quarantine cross on the door. Or she will be hanged for the hanging of the guard. Yes, they will most certainly die. But my brother and I will live. I will make sure of that.

I reach over and take his hand.

"Let's walk along the river," I say. "I want to feel the great coldness under the soles of my feet."

1677

The artist is at work on two paintings. One is a scene in the Arctic with a floundering ship pitched steeply among the ice floes, the other a painting of the frozen Thames.

The artist is from Holland, but he has spent a great deal of his life in England. He is an etcher as well as a painter and most of his work features animals – dogs and hunting scenes – so he is almost unaware of the fact that he has painted animals in both the Arctic scene and the painting of the frozen Thames. In the former a team of wild dogs chases a man across the ice in the foreground. In the Thames painting a dog barks at two men who have fallen to the ice, also in the foreground.

The painting of the frozen Thames is huge, almost six feet wide, and it shows practically the entire span of the London Bridge in its background.

The main action of the painting is a line of figures advancing across the river from a set of stairs at the left. The stairs are from a ferry stage and, since the watermen can't row people across the ice, they stand guard at the top of the stairs and charge people to walk down the flight of steps onto the icy river. Once the people walk across they will be charged again to climb the steps on the other side.

All of the figures are men except for one woman in the left background who is walking over the ice with a tray of cups balanced on her head. The painter has been down numerous times to the Thames and knows that, during this winter's freeze, there is brandy for sale out on the ice.

There are two references to the painter's home-land in the painting of the Thames. One is a figure of a skater in the bottom right corner, wearing a Dutch hat. The second is a sign for an inn hanging at the top of the stairs. The sign has the drawing of a Dutch hat inside a wreath.

The figures in the painting are very active, help-ing each other over the ice, throwing snowballs, skating. One man shoots a gun at some birds crossing the sky over the bridge.

In the Arctic painting there are fewer people. The central space of the painting is taken up with the distressed ship, sails up and flapping, tossed high by the ice floes. The background is merely a horizon line and there are only a handful of men and the wild dogs in the foreground.

They seem like very different paintings, and it is only when they are both near completion that the painter realizes that they are very much alike. The scenes might be different, but the ice in both paint-ings is the same ice. It occupies the same space and looks identical in both depictions – chunks of sheared white more than six feet high, with chasms and craters, rivers of clearer, darker ice running under the base of the ice cliffs.

The painter steps back, walks across the floor of his studio, and looks at the paintings from the far wall. He has never been to the Arctic, but he has been down to the Thames every afternoon all this long winter. Of course he would end up painting the same picture. He squints at the paintings. It is the Thames that looks fantastical, the ice so huge and difficult. The Arctic picture, this place he has never been and will never be, and which he has modelled solely on the vision of the frozen Thames – the Arctic painting looks exactly right, looks real.

1684

—

An entire village has been built upon the ice. Booths have been made from blankets and the oars of the watermen. The main thoroughfare between the booths has been named Freezland Street. There are coffee houses and taverns, booths that sell slabs of roast beef. An ox has been roasted whole, and a printing press has been set up so that one can have one's name printed in this place *where men so oft were drowned*. The Frost Fair is visited by a royal party that includes King

Charles II (in what will be the last week of his life). They have their names engraved on a card *Printed by G. Groom, on the ICE, on the River Thames, January 31, 1684.*

It is the coldest winter there has ever been and the ice freezes hard and fast and smooth. The watermen trade their boats for sledges and pull people across the river, for the same price as when they had rowed them over. A whirly sledge twirls passengers around a stake set into the ice. Coaches are pulled by both horses and men. There are games of football and bowls, horse and donkey races. There is music and a large bear garden. A fox is hunted on the ice and a bull is staked out in a ring by the Temple Stairs. Dogs are tossed in to bait the bull and many are gored to death before the beast is brought down. Men have skates to slide over the river, and horses have their hooves wrapped in linen to prevent this very same thing. Three cannons are brought out upon the ice to commemorate the royal visit, and boats are sent over the frozen Thames with their sails set and wheels fastened to their hulls to keep them upright.

The Frost Fair is also called a Blanket Fair, on account of the blankets used to fashion the booths. The Fair lasts eight weeks and what is remarkable about it is not the city of wonders that it produces. It is not the fact that the winter of 1684 is so cold that trees split apart suddenly, as though struck by lightning; or that the river ice on the Thames freezes to a depth of eleven inches. It is not even that a printing press was hauled out onto the ice, that words were formed from the mouth of winter, that men and women can have their names printed in a place that, by spring, will cease to exist. No, what is remarkable about the Frost Fair is that it does not operate by the same rules that govern life on land. It is a phenomenon and is therefore free of the laws and practices of history. The poor and the rich alike inhabit the same space, participate in the same sports and diversions, are, for a very brief moment in time, equal citizens of a new and magical world.

1689

These freezes are going to kill me. It's bad enough that I am one of four thousand watermen plying trade on the river Thames, trying to row twopence out of the pockets of the wealthy men. It's bad enough that the hay and straw boatmen have started to carry passengers, even though they are not licensed to do so and we, as freemen, have had to apprentice for seven long years to be granted this right. It's bad enough that we live on the south bank of the river because the theatres were here and we used to row the traffic from the city side to the theatres before the theatres up and moved to the north side of the river. It's bad enough that our numbers are kept unreasonably high because we're used as naval reserve and, anytime there's a war on, we can be plucked from our spot on the river and pressed into service for our country and King. I am not ashamed to say that I have hidden myself away to avoid being sent into battle.

We are working men, but we have a history and tradition, a certain respectability. We wear a dignified red coat with our numbered silver licence pinned to our sleeve. The wherries we row across the river are painted red or green, to distinguish them from other boats. We even have our own coat of arms, with a pair of oars overtop a boat bobbing on the water and two giant seahorses standing sentinel on either side of the boat. There is a school for watermen to be opened in Putney by one Thomas Martyn, a man who was rescued from the river by one of us.

All of this to lament the fate of the watermen

during these freezes of the Thames. I am, simply put, starving because the river has turned to ice. At first I tried to transform my wherry into a sledge, to pull people across the river, but I cannot pull much faster than a man can walk, and the custom I received was so little as to be not worth the effort. It is far more exhausting to pull a boat over the ice than it is to row one that same distance over water. When the river is in its natural state, the only way across is by the London Bridge, and that is so clogged with traffic that it is a much slower prospect than being ferried across the water. In this way I make my living, because of this situation. Now the situation has completely changed. The entire river has become a bridge and a man may simply walk from one side of the Thames to the other if he wishes to cross it.

I cannot be a waterman without water.

Every morning I walk from my house on the south bank to the stairs where I used to row out across the river. I'm there by seven, walk up and down the stairs for warmth, stand on the landing stage, and smoke my pipe. This early in the morning there is not a soul

out on the ice, but if I look to my left and right I can see the other watermen standing on their landing stages. We are like sentries, on guard over our precious Thames, and all of us waiting for the same thing – for the morning when the ice begins to shift and crack and the river is returned to us again.

1691

The ice can barely hold us up. The freeze was sudden and the thaw has been just as sudden. We are more than halfway across the river now, so there is no going back, but when I turn to see how far we've come, I can see that the prints of my boots are slowly filling up with water behind me.

I was warned by my husband not to attempt a crossing. *The ice has crept over the river while we slept*, he said. *It could creep away again, just as swiftly.* But my husband has been wrong about many things and I chose not to believe him. When the river froze in 1684, there was a Frost Fair on it for weeks and the ice held and held. A cannon was wheeled onto that ice and booths set up in the middle of the Thames. I looked out of the window this morning and saw this ice, and I thought of that ice.

But I am learning that each ice, each freeze, is different from the one before. That freeze was hard and smooth. This one is uneven, spongy underfoot, covered with snow. I cannot even see the ice itself and so only half believe that it is there. But when I turned and saw my footprints filling with water, I knew that, not only is the ice there, but the river is there as well.

I am taking my son to Cheapside Street to buy him some boots. He has grown fast, and his old ones are worn through at the toes. There is a good shoemaker on Cheapside who will not charge us very much to make Jack a new pair of boots.

I thought it would be easier to cross the river over the ice instead of trying to cross at the bridge. The bridge is always so full of people and carts, and the river was empty of traffic this morning.

Now I know why this is so.

"Mama," says Jack. "My feet are getting wet."

The water is over his boots.

"Walk behind me," I say. "A little ways behind me."

I pick my way carefully over the ice, testing each spot where I am to place my foot, treading gently on the surface so as not to disturb it. My boy is lighter than I am. If I do not go through the ice, then he will be safe walking behind me. Neither of us knows how to swim.

I am all over shivering with fear. All I want is for us to make it safely to the other side. I will never be so foolish again. I will listen to my husband. I will never trust in something that seems one way but is another. Ice is water. Water cannot hold anything up.

I look down and see the mush of snow and the wet leather of my boots. I look up and see the spire of St. Antholin's church in Watling Street. It glitters in the sunlight, a tall needle piercing the sky. I will thread my fear to that spire, sew myself in towards land by that needle. Just in thinking this I can feel my hope grow taut, feel it tug me onwards to the church.

St. Antholin's was named after a monk who supposedly lived to be 105 years old. It is a new church, built to take the place of one that burned in the Great Fire of 1666. King Charles's architect, Christopher Wren, has been working on it for thirteen years. This is the year it will finally be finished.

Jack is thirteen years old. I gave birth to him during the same month that the building of St. Antholin's began, and I have always linked the two events together. Nothing bad will happen to us as long as I can keep the church spire in my sights, as long as I can keep us walking over the Thames towards it.

Perhaps this is the nature of ice, that it is an illusion. Perhaps ice is merely a form of faith. Step onto the water. Believe that it will hold you up, that you may walk safely across it, that it is strong enough to carry you – and it will.

1695

I am looking out the window of this shop, down at the frozen river, at the spot where my mother and I nearly drowned four years ago.

In all that time the Thames has been water and now it is ice again. This year was a very cold winter, the coldest that anyone can remember. It is said that it is so cold that wine will freeze in a glass at the supper table.

The river has been frozen for more than a week now, but I will not venture out across it. I will never walk out over that ice again.

All the same, I cannot stop watching it. When there are no customers in the shop, I come up here, to the top floor of the house, and I look out over the white world of the river. People and carts move across the frozen surface, move from one side of the river to the other as though it were the easiest passage in the world.

I remember how there was no one on the river that morning my mother and I started across. I thought, how lucky we were to have the space all to ourselves. It was only when I noticed my mother looking around in a fearful sort of way that I knew that it was not a good thing that we were alone out there.

My boots sunk into the ice and my feet became wet and I thought we were to drown. My mother bade me follow her, and I did this, but I did not trust that we would make it to shore.

When we had made it to shore, I refused to leave it. I would not travel back with my mother to our house on the south side of the river. I would not cross that water again, even over the London Bridge. That whole day she tried to persuade me to return, but I would not, and so my mother helped me find a shop that would have me as an apprentice. This is the shop. I am now finished my apprenticeship and have qualified as a fruiterer. The man I apprenticed for, Geoffrey, has taken me on as a partner in his business. That is him now, stomping about downstairs. In winter, and with the Thames frozen, there is not much fruit for selling. Apples. We have apples. Geoffrey must be moving the baskets of apples from one side of the shop to the other.

From the upstairs window the frozen Thames looks like a swan's wing, a white curve of feather and bone. It looks beautiful and harmless, and I know that neither is true.

That's Geoffrey's heavy tread on the stairs and there he is, standing at the top of the staircase, his red beard stuck with sawdust. He is carrying an armful of bricks.

"Help me," he says, as he leans forward and spills his load of bricks onto the floor.

"Help you with what?"

"We're going to brick up the windows," says Geoffrey. "Now that Mary's dead the King is intending to raise revenues."

Geoffrey was partial to Queen Mary. She governed with King William and now William alone is in charge of the realm.

"And?" I say. Geoffrey is a nice man, but he is a tad parsimonious with the words.

"And he's planning a window tax. Every window in every building is to be taxed."

I can see that this makes a certain kind of sense. The richer the man, the bigger the house and the more windows he is likely to have in that house.

Geoffrey kicks the bricks rather angrily towards me. "I'm going to brick up these windows," he says. "These ones, up here. Only the shop window downstairs needs to stay." He turns to go back down for more bricks. "Help me," he says, over his shoulder.

We sleep in these rooms above the shop. It will be like sleeping in a tomb, with the windows all bricked up.

I lean forward, press my forehead against the cold glass. This is how it would feel to lay my face against the river ice. It would be this hard and chill, this smooth against my skin.

I still dream about that day I walked out over the ice with my mother. In the dream I am following her and she is walking slowly down into the water. In the dream I am not afraid.

1709

—

The woman waits for her husband at the side of the road. She carries a length of new rope and an orange and she has wrapped herself in two shawls against the cold. She is early, but she was so afraid of being late that she hurried quicker than she knew she could through the frigid streets to wait here.

Her husband is being taken by open cart from Newgate Prison to Tyburn to hang at the gallows there. He has been caught thieving and has been sentenced to death.

The woman stamps her feet to shake the cold out of them. It is all due to the coldness of the winter that her husband was caught and tried and now is being taken to the gibbet. The winter is so cold that the Thames has frozen over and many cattle and birds have perished.

The woman's husband had a pet sparrow. He had found it fallen from its nest when it was a fledgling and he had fed it and kept it tucked in the pocket of his coat. He taught it to come to his whistle and then he set his plan to working. He walked about London, looking in the windows of the fancy houses until he saw something he wanted – some silver plate that could be sold and melted down – and then he opened a window and released the sparrow into the house. The bird flew from room to room and if the man heard no screams or shouts then he knew that the house was empty and he would follow the bird through the window and steal the plate. If he were caught in the house he would say that he had followed his pet sparrow in and was after catching it, and to show that the bird was indeed a pet he would have it return to his whistle.

This plan never failed, and the man and his wife enjoyed a comfortable life from the profits of this enterprise. They bought the finest cuts of meat and had their clothes made by the best tailor and dressmaker in the city. The sparrow was fed cream and bread milled from the choicest flour.

But this winter proved to be too cold for the little bird. It died one night, fell from its perch in the parlour of the house where the man and woman lived, and they found its small frozen body the next morning when they woke. It was the bird that had protected the thief, and the mistake the man made was in not realizing this soon enough. The very next house he entered to rob he was caught in.

There is a clatter of wheels on the cobblestones and the hanging cart swings into view from around the corner. The woman steps out to meet it, forces the driver to stop his horses.

"I need to speak with my husband," she says, and

gestures to the back of the cart where her husband sits on the boards dressed in his best suit and guarded by a man with a pike.

"You may come along if you wish," says the driver, and the guard helps the woman climb up into the wagon.

The woman sits down beside her husband.

"I brought you a rope," she says.

"No need," he says. "The sheriff supplies the hanging rope."

"Well, I wasted twopence then."

"Perhaps your second husband will be able to make use of it," says the man, and they both smile.

"I brought you an orange too," she says, handing it to him. His hands are tied in front of him and they make a nest for the orange to sit in.

"Where did you get an orange at this time of year?" says the guard.

"The fruiterer down by the river has some from a Spanish ship."

"Must have cost you dear," says the guard.

"I can peel it for you," says the woman.

"No," says her husband. "I like the look of it." They both look down into his cupped hands at the orange, bright like a flame in this white world.

There is nothing that can be said between them that has not already been said. Now it remains simply for the man to die well, to die bravely. His wife will help with this by tugging on his feet as he hangs from the gibbet, to hasten his death. Then his body will be cut down and claimed by the anatomists for dissection. But the woman has the last of her money tucked down the front of her dress and she plans to buy the body of her husband from these doctors before they can chop it up. She will buy his body and have it buried entire.

For now there is nothing but this bumpy ride over the cobbles to Tyburn. There is the warmth of this man she loves pressed against the side of her body, and there is this orange, bright and glorious, roosting in the safe hollow of his hands.

1716

Bess is exhausted. She has been rhyming all day and all the words have left her body, lifted like a flock of birds into the sky.

"I need to stop," she says to her husband, Will, but he has moved out of hearing, is well out in front of the booth, trying to entice customers in to see her.

The river has been frozen for almost two months and a town of tents has been erected upon it. There is a cook's tent where gentlemen come to dine every evening. There are tents that sell ale and tents that sell gingerbread. There are two printing presses and people can have their names printed on a card to keep for posterity. An ox has been roasted near the Hungerford Stairs by a descendant of the man who roasted an ox on the ice at the last Frost Fair in 1684. A woman selling apples has fallen through the ice and drowned and has been immortalized in a poem, two lines of which Bess is wildly jealous of: *The cracking crystal yields; she sinks she dies,/Her head chopt off from her lost shoulders flies.*

Will and Bess's booth has a sign out front that reads: *Rhiming on the Hard Frost.* Bess has always had the gift of rhyme, and it was Will's idea to turn it into money at the Frost Fair. So far they have been rather alarmingly successful. A customer will offer up a line and Bess will complete the poem. If the customer cannot think of a line Bess's husband will supply one. This is a better situation for Bess as Will gives her the first line to a poem she has already invented and memorized. Unfortunately most customers prefer to give their own first lines.

While Bess is reciting the poem, Will will copy it

AND YE FED ME · NAKED AND YE
HUNGRY AND · CLOTHED ME

Upon the Frost in the Year 1715-6.

Behold the Liquid Thames now frozen or'e,
That lately Ships of mighty Burthen bore!
The Watermen for want of Rowing Boats,
Make use of Booths to get their Pence and Groats.
Here you may see Beef Roasted on the Spit,
And for your Money you may taste a bit.
There you may print your Name, tho' cannot write,
'Cause num'd with Cold: 'Tis done with great Delight
And lay it by, that Ages yet to come,
May see what Things upon the Ice were done.

From the Printing-house, Bow-Church-Yard.

Mrs Anne Robins

Printed upon the Ice on the Thames, at the
Maidenhead, the Second Booth, at Old
Swan Stairs, Jan. 14. 1715-6.

down and then presents the copy to the customer to keep as a memento.

Most of the first lines have to do with the ice. *What wondrous magic the ice on the Thames doth be*, to which Bess followed with, *The river enslaved, but the people of London set free.* But over the course of the days and weeks she has made every possible rhyme and really there are just so many words that will match up with *ice*. She is tired of *nice* and *price* and *concise*. She is sick to death of *thrice* and *dice* and *wise*, which she pronounces as *wice* to get the rhyme.

"I need a rest," she says to Will, who has returned to the booth and has, she sees too late, returned with a man in a top hat.

"What?" says Will.

"This day I trod upon the ice," says the man.

Bess could scream. She could open her mouth and tip her head back and scream until her voice shredded in her throat.

Will and the customer look at her expectantly.

"This day I trod upon the ice," says the man again, helpfully.

Bess is tired of being an oddity. Her gift has made her little better than a performing dog. It has not done her any good at all. The money they earn, Will spends at the ale tent. She is freezing cold from being all day out on the river. This is not how she wants to live.

The only way out of somewhere is by the door you came in.

"This day I trod upon the ice," she says. "I paid and paid a dreadful price./I will not pretend that this is nice./A poet as whore will not suffice."

1740

———

The winter is full of malice. This is how it seems. The river is choked with icebergs, the rugged chunks of ice growing more immense each day as the ice is broken up every twelve hours by the high tides, refreezing as the water ebbs and creating a spectacular ice field as a result of all the tumult. Several people fall through the ice and drown as the surface looks solid but is really too weak in places to be safely walked upon. A

Frost Fair has been established on the most stable section of the Thames.

The winter is so cold that passengers being rowed across the open portions of the river have perished while sitting in the wherries. Post boys have died from the cold while riding out on horseback. A woman with a baby is found dead, her living child still suckling at her frozen breast. Farmers spend their time breaking the ice on the troughs so their animals can drink. Ale and wine freeze, and even bottles of ink in the drawing-rooms of houses turn to ice.

All those who depend on the river and the good weather for their livelihoods begin to starve. They parade through the streets of London – the watermen, fishermen, carpenters, gardeners – carrying the tools of their trade and dragging a peter-boat, singing dirges for their lost wages and begging for relief money.

Ice stops the words from flowing to the page; the wine flowing to the glass. The line cannot drop to

catch a fish. The vegetables and fruit will not grow in the frozen earth.

The winter is not just cold in England. In Russia, the Empress Anne has an ice palace constructed with walls that are three feet thick and all the furniture – beds and chairs and tables – made of ice.

The thaw of the Thames goes just as badly as the freeze. It comes fierce and sudden, huge slabs of ice crashing through the arches of London Bridge, damaging the bridge and carrying away portions of the Frost Fair. Booths and huts, upright and unmanned on their ice floes, hurtle downstream, some with their signs still attached to the front of the structure. It is as though the people of London need reminding that the river is a wild thing and this cannot be forgotten because, if it is, the Thames will simply arch its back and throw anything off that tries to tame it.

1762

—

COLD, kold. *a.* [Sax.] Not hot; not warm; gelid. *Milton.* Causing sense of cold. *Milton.* Chill; shivering; frigid. *Hooker.* Unaffecting. *B. Jonson.* Reserved; coy. *Shak.* Chaste. *Shak.* Not welcome. *Shak.* Not hasty; not violent. Not affecting the scent strongly. *Shak.* Not having the scent strongly affected. *Shakespeare.*

To FREEZE, freeze. *v.a.* pret. *froze.* [*vrieson*, Dutch] To be congealed with cold. *Ray.* To be of that degree of cold by which water is congealed. *Shakespeare.*

To FREEZE, freeze. *v.a.* pret. *froze.* part. *Frozen, or froze.* To congeal with cold. *Milton.* To kill by cold. *Shak.* To chill by the loss of power or motion. *Shakespeare.*

FRIGID, frid-jid. 544. *a.* [*frigidus*, Lat.] Cold; wanting warmth. *Cheyne.* Wanting warmth of affection. Impotent; without warmth of body. Dull; without fire of fancy. *Tatler.*

FRIGORIFICK, fri-go-rif-ik. *a.* [*frigorificus*, Lat.] Causing cold. *Quincy.*

FROST, frost. *n.s.* [Sax.] The last effect of cold; the power or act of congelation. *South.* The appearance of plants and trees sparkling with congelation of dew. *Pope.*

FROSTNAIL, frost-nale. *n.s.* A nail with a prominent head driven into the horse's shoes, that it may pierce the ice. *Grew.*

FROSTY, fros-te. *a.* Having the power of congelation; excessive cold. *Bacon.* Chill in affection; without warmth of kindness or courage. *Shak.* Hoary; grey-haired; resembling frost. *Shakespeare.*

FROZEN, fro-zn. 103. *part. pass.* of *freeze.* Congealed with cold. *Dryden.* Chill in affection. *Sidney.* Void of heat or appetite. *Pope.*

ICE, ise. *n.s.* [Sax.] Water or other liquor made solid by cold. *Shak.* Concreted sugar. – *To break the ice.* To make the first opening to any attempt. *Shakespeare.*

ICICLE, i-sik-kl. 405. *n.s.* [from ice] A shoot of ice commonly hanging down from the upper part. *Brown.*

ICKLE, ik-kl. *n.s.* In the north of England, an icicle. *Grose.*

ICY, i-se. *a.* Full of ice; covered with ice; made of ice; cold; frosty. *Shak.* Cold; free from passion. *Shak.* Frigid; backward. *Shakespeare.*

RIVER, riv-ur. 98. *n.s.* [*rivière*, Fr.; *rivus*, Lat.] A land current of water bigger than a brook. *Locke.*

To THAW, thaw. 466. *v.n.* [Sax.] To grow liquid after congelation; to melt. *Donne.* To remit the cold which had caused frost.

WINTER, win-tur. 98. *n.s.* [Sax.; *winter,* Dan., Germ., and Dutch.] The cold season of the year. *Sidney.*

To WINTER, win-tur. *v.n.* To pass the winter. *Isiah, xviii.*

To WINTER, win-tur. *v.a.* To feed or manage in the winter. *Temple.*

WINTER is often used in composition.

1768

___

Arthur Young cannot get warm. He walks from the bed to the desk, to the window and then back to the bed, to the door and then back to the window. If he stops he starts to feel his limbs stiffening up. If he increases his pace around the room he crashes into the furniture. He wears all his clothes, including his heavy outdoor coat. The thin spew of smoke issuing from the coal fire in the corner of the room does absolutely nothing to warm it. Last night the bedclothes were so cold that Arthur felt he was actually lying under slabs of ice.

From the window the frozen Thames sparkles in the noon sun. *The hottest part of the day,* Arthur reminds himself as he crosses from the window to the door.

He is in London to meet with his publisher. His book, *A Six Weeks' Tour Through the Southern Counties of England and Wales,* is due out this spring and he has had to make some final alterations to the text. The book is the culmination of a walk through the agricultural land of southern England. Arthur is interested in agricultural practices and decided to simply wander about and record what he saw in terms of soil, crops, roads, cattle, farm-buildings, methods of farming. He is also working on a book about his own experiments with agriculture, but he can sense already that his walking tour will be the better book. Sometimes the simplest idea is the strongest one.

Arthur Young has taken a while to find his way to

writing about agriculture. He is the son of a rector, was sent to school to learn commerce but showed no aptitude for it. He wrote a pamphlet on the war in North America when he was seventeen and started a periodical called *The Universal Museum*, which he stopped at the advice of Samuel Johnson. In the few short years after that he wrote four novels and a book on politics, but none of them came to much. When his father died he was left a small estate bridled with debt. He tried farming his mother's property and then married Miss Alien, a woman he is not particularly happy with and isn't sure he even loves. In 1766, he rented a hundred acres in Hertfordshire to try his farming experiments on. So far all his experiments have failed. The land he has rented is so poor that it threatens to defeat him. He has written about the place to a friend: "I know not what epithet to give this soil; sterility falls short of the idea; a hungry vitriolic gravel."

Arthur should feel utterly devastated at this point in his life, but he actually feels quite buoyant, and as long as he keeps moving briskly around his room at the inn, he need not fear that he will freeze to death today.

He has liked walking through England and writing about the farms and farmers he has found there. He plans to do a walking tour of the north and east and west to complete the survey of the countryside, once the book on the southern sojourn has been published. The summers will be for walking and the winters will be for writing.

Arthur makes another circumnavigation of his room. This time he stops at the window and looks down at the Thames. It still astonishes him to see it frozen. But perhaps even a river needs to rest and, like a garden asleep in winter, will come back stronger because of the pause. Perhaps ice is a kind of sleep.

And looking down at the flat, blank white of the river, Arthur Young thinks something else as well. The small black figures moving along the smooth expanse look exactly like words, exactly like words being set down upon a page.

1776

I have to warm my tools in the fire just so I can hang on to them. My hands turn into blocks of stone holding the chisel and hammer, and the actual block of stone I am carving is as cold to the touch as a block of ice.

My breath is as thick around me as fog. This morning when I rose, ice had formed in a crust under my bed. All around my London house the birds are falling frozen from the skies, or swooping weakly down to eat the steaming dung the horses have left in the streets. The horses themselves are so hungry that they have started coming into the gardens and scratching through the frost and snow to eat any of the plants that might be growing there.

In the south a whole flock of sheep was buried in the snow for thirteen days before a dog managed to find them, all somehow still alive.

The river is a block of ice and the ferrymen cannot work. Like the horses, they scrape about for money and food. A great many people are unable to work because of the cold and the frozen river. I must be one of the lucky ones in that regard, for people are always dying in frigid winters, and the dead always need a stone above their heads to mark their graves.

This is what I am doing, carving words into a stone for someone who perished in this cold weather.

I work in the front room of an old house on the south bank of the Thames. I work with the doors open because of the stone dust – how it makes me choke if there is not enough fresh air about – how it crawls into every part of my hair and clothing, every nook and cranny of the house.

From the open doors I can see the river, can see

the skaters carving marks into the surface of the ice, as I am carving words into this stone. The Thames has become a tomb, a gravestone for the river that lies beneath. The river that has been buried alive.

I like what I do. It is good, honest work. I like the effort of chiselling words into stone, of writing, for the last time, the name of the man or woman or child who has died. There is a solemnity about the act of carving the name that I appreciate. It takes work and it should. Leaving this world should not be an easy thing, should not be without effort.

Because I have carved so many names, and because it takes so long to carve them, I have remembered every one. They live on in my fingertips, in the brush of my hand over stone. All these people I never knew who have become, in death, members of my own family.

But in all the years I have been making tomb-stones, I have never made one so strange as this. It almost seems a jest, what this boy's family have desired me say upon his stone; but I know, having met the family, that they are as upset as any other family about the death of their son. Because his death, the manner of his death, was so strange, they do not know what else to say about it.

Living so close by the river as I do, I have heard the noises the water makes from underneath the ice. It groans like a living creature. I hear it at night, late at night when the streets are quiet. I turn in my cold bed and the river turns in hers, and she lets out a moan as she does it.

I am not alarmed by this. The noise of the river is an odd comfort. It makes me feel not so alone.

I put down the chisel and the hammer, shake the cold from my numb fingers, and stand back to admire my work. It is done. Another soul is stitched to the earth.

> *In memory of the Clerk's son,*
> *Bless my i, i, i, i, i, i,*
> > *Here I lies*
> > *In a sad pickle*
> > *Killed by an icicle,*
> *In the year of Anno Domini 1776.*

1784

—

Another cold winter. More have perished this year – frozen by the side of the road, buried under drifts of snow – than in any year in living memory.

It only makes good sense to stay indoors.

It only makes good sense to find an occupation to fully engage the body and the mind whilst remaining indoors.

I am fully engaged in perfecting the recipe for Jugged Hare. For years I have just made it as I felt, using whatever was on hand and not thinking of how to improve the quality of the taste. Now that I have this forced time indoors I am able to experiment. The cold, however, does interfere with my supply of hares. My husband is kept busy on our small acreage, chasing them through the frosted fields. He has even ventured as far as the frozen Thames in pursuit of a fitting rabbit for my pot.

They are scrawny creatures, these winter hares that he hunts down and brings to me. They always need a little extra stewing to persuade the stringy meat from their bones.

JUGGED HARE

– *one jointed hare*
– *a fistful of flour*
– *bacon drippings*
– *onions cut in slices*
– *a jar of chopped bacon*
– *some game stock*
– *a spoon of ground cloves*
– *a handful of mixed sweet herbs*
– *a sprinkle of mace*

1. Flour the hare and brown in the bacon drippings. Remove the pieces when they are browned and add the onions. Brown them also, and then add the bacon.

2. Return the hare to the pot with the stock, cloves, herbs, and mace.

3. Boil the lot, then simmer for three hours – longer if the hare is old or thin   until the meat is tender.

My husband has become an expert on *Hasenpfeffer*, as skilled as I am. He sits down every evening with his napkin tucked under his chin. He takes the first bite and shifts the meat from one side of his mouth to the other. Often I cannot wait for his verdict.

"Well?" I say. "Too much mace? Not enough cloves? Too long in the pot?"

My husband is interested primarily in the rabbit, for this has been where he has put his attention. While I have been adding and removing herbs, sifting just the right amount of flour over the pieces of the hare, he has been chasing the beast through the cold winter fields, running his dogs to it, racing behind on his favourite horse. It is the rabbit and the rabbit only that he sits in judgment of every evening.

"I knew this was a plump one," he will say. "I knew it when I first spied it in the stubble. I knew the meat would be this tender, would slip so softly from the bone. Last night's rabbit was hard to chew but this one – this one is just right."

1789

—

The freezing of the Thames always occurs above London Bridge because the bridge acts as a dam and the water moves slower above the dam than below it.

But this year the temperature dropped so low in December and remained so through January, that the river froze all the way from Putney to a mile below London Bridge at Rotherhithe.

There is another Frost Fair, this one more

—

elaborate than usual. There are puppet shows and roundabouts. A young bear is hunted on the ice at Rotherhithe. Pigs and sheep are roasted whole.

The publican and his wife have been out on the ice, enjoying all the diversions for one whole afternoon. They have left the pub in the charge of their son and daughter and are now making their way back to it over the river. The evening will be busy and they want to be back in time to take full advantage of the lucky fact that their pub is right beside the Thames at Rotherhithe.

It has been a good afternoon. The publican and his wife have laughed together and felt an ease they haven't remembered feeling since they were first married. Even though they are in a hurry they walk slowly back through the fair. The publican's wife holds her husband's arm, likes the feeling of it tucked tight against her ribs.

"Look at that," says the publican. They stop in front of a small wooden booth. There is a sign tacked on to the front of the hut: *This Booth to Let. The present possessor of the Premises is Mr. Frost. His*

affairs, however, not being on a permanent footing, a
dissolution, or bankruptcy may soon be expected, and
a final settlement of the whole entrusted to Mr. Thaw.

The publican's wife is finished reading the sign well before the publican. For the first time she wonders if perhaps she is possessed of more brain than her husband, and this thought makes her even more fond of him.

The pub is full of customers by the time they return to it. All evening the publican and his wife rush about, serving ale and food, sopping up spilled beer, putting more coal on the two fires that burn either side of the downstairs bar. It is only after the last man is ushered out of the pub to the winter darkness and the publican has bolted and locked the door that they have the opportunity to speak to one another again.

"What a day," says the publican. He has lit the candle for bed and is standing behind his wife on the staircase. "Why did you stop?" he says. "Are you not as tired out as I am?"

The publican's wife is looking at the cable that

attaches to the main beam of the pub's ceiling and runs out the front window. "Do you think we should ask the Captain to release us?" she says. "It's been weeks now. Surely the ice will be about breaking up soon."

All the ships have frozen solid into the river ice. There are no moorings to attach lines to, no water to drop anchor in. One enterprising captain, fearing the ice would melt and he wouldn't be aboard his vessel at the time of melting, has fastened a cable around the beam of the pub and attached the other end to his ship. He has also deposited the ship's anchor in the pub cellar, with the anchor chain leading through a cellar window and back to the ship.

The publican has had a good day, but it has been a long day, and he just cannot be about doing even one more thing before bed. "Tomorrow," he says, and he nudges his wife's behind and half pushes her up the stairs.

It is the moaning that wakes the publican's wife. At first she thinks her husband is having a bad dream, dreaming he is the bear pursued on the ice by hunters. She lays a hand on his shoulder to wake him. But no, the noise isn't a human noise. The noise is the groans of her house being pulled apart.

The publican's wife leaps out of bed and rushes to the window. Down on the river the ice has cracked apart and shifted. She can see the black shine of open water. The ship that is anchored to their house is floating free once again.

"What?" says the publican, sitting bolt upright in bed.

His wife doesn't even have time to turn around and tell him what has happened before the house collapses on top of them and kills them.

1795

The ice was bad. The floods are worse. Now that there has been a thaw the ice has broken up and the tides carry the huge floes up and down the river. Boats are cut from their moorings and driven against the pilings of the bridge. The ice floes jam up in places and flood the buildings along the shore. The streets are canals. In some of the flooded large country houses downriver the people in the houses travel from room to room by boat.

Seven men have died this winter from falling through the ice, and the body of a man who had gone over the side of a boat was swept through the arches of the bridge, completely encased in ice.

I had the good idea of blowing up the ice that has dammed against the south bank and threatens to flood the houses there. It was a very good idea while I was sitting in the pub having a glass of ale with my friends. It has lost a bit of its appeal now that I am rowing the explosives out towards the ice floes in a borrowed wherry.

The gunpowder is wrapped in oilskins to protect it from the wet. I plan on setting it in the middle of the floes, igniting the fuse, and then rowing quickly away.

It is harder than I'd thought to row through the blocks of ice. I keep crashing into them, alter my course accordingly, only to find that the floes have altered their course as well and I am liable to crash back into the same piece of ice a great many times before being able to squeeze past it.

It is also colder than I'd expected out on the river

and my gloveless hands are numb where they grip the ends of the oars.

I am the only person out on the icy arctic ocean of the Thames. My friends who encouraged me to do this whilst we were drinking ale in the public house, saw me grimly off from the Hungerford Stairs, not a one of them showing the enthusiasm of a few nights ago. I am the only one among us who has the courage to see a thing through.

"You'll surely be drowned," said Rupert, as he flung the painter into the boat and pushed it, rather savagely, away from shore.

I don't think that I will be drowned, but I do worry that I'll freeze to death here at the oars. Best to just get this finished. I can't wait for the perfect position for setting the explosives. Where I am will have to do. I nudge the boat up against a chunk of ice, throw the weighted length of rope out onto the ice surface to hold the boat, and wrestle the oilskin of gunpowder onto the floe.

My hands are so cold that it takes a few attempts to light the match and ignite the fuse. Only when it's burning nicely, sputtering slowly to its end, do I realize that my boat has drifted away. It is bobbing peacefully among the distant ice floes, well out of my reach.

My friends are watching from the shore. They will see my predicament, will see me as I plunge desperately into the icy river, and they will think that their warnings were correct. They might not even be that sorry that I have died, so righteous will they be in thinking I went foolishly and needlessly to my grave.

The water is so cold that it burns like fire. It scalds my skin and knocks the breath from me as I struggle to get away from the explosives. The fuse hisses on the ice behind me like a snake.

I am not a good swimmer, but I am propelled by the fear of death and that does remarkable things for my abilities. I race through the water as fast as a bird slices through air, trying to move as quickly as I can before my arms go completely numb.

I can see my friends on the shore of the river. They are waving stupidly, as though to warn me that I am in danger of drowning, as though they can tell me a thing I do not already know. I can hear the fuse burning down. I want to look behind me, but I do not dare in case I am not as far away from the oilskin of explosives as I think. I don't want to know if I am to die.

But it seems that luck finds me on the river. Just when I think I can swim no farther, I feel hands pulling me from the water, feel the rough bilge of a boat against my cheek. Someone forces my mouth open, none too gently, and pours a coughing amount of brandy down my throat. Someone else wraps me in a blanket.

I hear the explosives and, as I struggle to sit upright in the boat, I see the great wave rise up before me, rise up and bear down towards the south bank, surge towards the exact spot where my friends are waiting on the shore.

1796

The colder it gets, the better I like it. I love that there is a thick frost on the inside of my windows, and that the glass of water I left by my bed last night froze solid by morning. What I would really like is that I would wake with icicles hanging from my nose and ears.

I find the cold wholly inspirational. Every morning I tromp along the icy Thames and every afternoon I come back to my small room and try and write about it.

I want to compose a symphony for the frozen river. I want to write music to be played upon the ice, the way that Handel's "Water Music" was meant to be played upon the water of the Thames. I want to write something as magnificent as Purcell's "Cold Song," which included in the music the chattering of teeth.

My progress is slow.

I come from a family of musicians. My grandfather was one of the violinists in the orchestra that premiered the "Water Music," and my father, also a violinist, has played chamber music at Court. I can play most instruments tolerably well, but it is as a composer that I hope to make my name.

Two years ago I had a small gavotte published and I have heard that many still dance to its tune, although whenever I have myself gone to a dance I have never heard it played. Still, I expect it lingers well in memory and perhaps, while people listen to the music of others, they are really still hearing mine.

To have something played on the ice is a far superior idea to having a symphony played on the water. My grandfather told me of the troubles they had with Handel's piece. The main problem was the water itself. There were two barges that travelled together down the Thames in the summer of 1717. On one barge was King George I and members of his court. On the other barge was the fifty-piece orchestra. The King had requested this concert on the river. The barges were Handel's idea and the trouble was that they could not stay together, that the water moved them as it wanted and the music that was played was entirely dependent on the positioning of the boats. If the King's barge was close to the orchestra's barge, slow, soft music was played. If the barges were far apart then the orchestra sent out loud, brisk passages across the water.

With "Ice Music" there will be none of these concerns. The orchestra will sit on the frozen river and the audience will sit facing the music, just as if they were seated in the finest concert hall.

But as I have said, my progress is slow, and the chief reason for this is that the ice – my inspiration – also impedes my abilities. Simply put, it is so blasted cold that the ink congeals in my pen and the blood

congeals in my veins and I am possessed with a thick torpor of the mind that is, I believe, caused by the fact that I may be freezing to death. The brisk morning walks help, but when I sit down at my desk to compose in the afternoon, I have to be careful not to just lay my head down on my manuscript paper and fall straight asleep.

So far "Ice Music" has only two bars, and I don't really like one of them.

But what keeps me going is the river ice in the mornings when I walk out upon it. I like the sound of my boots on the snowy surface. I like the sound of the skaters and the horses' hooves and the cartwheels. The ice is a drum and everything resounds deeply upon its skin. This is what is in the first two bars of my symphony, this low, muffled thumping. I hope to return to it throughout the piece as a motif.

The musical notation looks like the river itself. The bar is the Thames, with banks on the outside and ripples of snow across the middle. The notes are skaters and walkers, horses and carts. Perhaps if I approached the page as I approach the river, walking up this bank and down that one, it would make a certain sense. Perhaps the music needs to make the same journey as the man and in this way it will sound true and lasting.

I blow on my hands and sit down; pick up my pen and begin to wander slowly up the frozen Thames.

1809

—

At first they seem like apples, each one fastened to the ground by a thin skin of ice. But as the miller's son begins to cross the field, he sees that this is not true. All around him, glittering like jewels in the early morning, is a flock of frozen birds.

Last night the rain fell as ice and the birds must have become coated with it, dropped from the sky to earth, and now they cannot open their ice-encrusted wings to fly. Without flight they are apples, they are stones, a field lit with bright stones.

The miller's son crouches down beside one of the birds. The black of its feathers glimmers through the ice. It is dead, he thinks. It has been sealed shut. He reaches out and pokes it with his finger and the lump of shiny coal shudders softly. He cups his hand around the bird and brings it close to his chest, breathes on it, until the warmth from his hands and the warmth from his breath melt the rind of ice around the rook and it stumbles away from him, stumbles and lifts clumsily up into the sky.

The boy walks through the field, warming each bird. Some are dead already, but many flicker back when he curls his hands around their frozen bodies. He counts them because the miller's son is used to counting, is good at it. There are twenty-seven rooks, ninety larks, a pheasant, and a buzzard hawk in that field, and the boy visits each one. It is late morning by the time he finishes his work and he stands in the wet grass, looking up, his cold hands pushed under his shirt, held tightly against his own bony chest.

In the sky above him are the birds he has freed, and the miller's son knows that he will never have a moment like this again, a moment when he is such glory.

The ice birds fell from the sky, he will say when he tells the story. *I breathed fire back into their bodies. My hands were an oven that warmed them. I set them to flying again.*

1811

—

All is madness. The King is locked in his private apartments at Windsor. The river is frozen solid. My brother has joined with the Luddites and is destroying the wool and cotton mills of Nottingham.

We can't move backwards. We can't move forwards. We are fastened in place, as the ice fastens the river.

King George III is mad. It is said that the recent

death of his daughter, Amelia, from tuberculosis has pushed him past the borders of sanity, but he has had episodes of madness before this. This one, though, is particularly bad. He has addressed parliament as "Lords and peacocks" and has spoken to people long dead. He imagines that London is flooded and claims to talk to angels. Someone told me he once greeted an oak tree as King Frederick of Prussia.

I have been fond of the King, the only monarch who has ruled during my lifetime. I like his interest in agriculture, like that he has gained the nickname of "Farmer George" because of this. When the great agriculture writer Arthur Young was working on his *Annals of Agriculture*, it is said the King furnished him with farming information under the pseudonym of Ralph Robinson.

Now Ralph is a prisoner in his own apartments. The Americans will be pleased with this. They have blamed him for all their problems when they were still a Colony.

The King is mad and yet no one must acknowledge it. Shakespeare's play *King Lear* has been banned from performance because his portrayal of a mad king is considered alarmingly similar to the real situation.

My brother is not mad, but he will surely be locked up for what he is doing in the north. One cannot wilfully destroy the instruments of progress just because they put honest working men out of jobs.

There is nothing I can do about my brother's beliefs or the mad King's conviction that he is communing with angels. The frozen river, however, I can have some effect on. I am making an ice road on which men and beasts may cross. Every day I walk the section of river that I have chosen for the construction of this road. I make sure it is still passable, that there are not places where the ice has begun to melt and the water burns through. I keep traffic moving over my portion of the river and in these times of uncertainty, this at least feels like I am doing something. This small act of movement feels like some sort of progress.

1814

—

The winter began with fog and ended with fire. During the last days of December 1813, the fog was so thick throughout London that

people carried lanterns in the daytime. Coachmen led their horses through the streets rather than risk overturning their coaches. Even those who knew the city well became lost in the labyrinth of streets during the days of the fog – *a darkness that can be felt.*

After the fog came the snow and the cold. For two days the snow fell; all traffic was impeded and great drifts rose like waves in the fields.

After the snow was a frost. Schools of fish called Golden Maids were washed ashore at Brighton. It is said they were blinded by the snow and had lost their way, had swum in the wrong direction and beached themselves instead of swimming out to sea.

After the frost came the cold. The river Thames froze solid and a Frost Fair was once again set up on the ice. The public way constructed between Blackfriars and London Bridge was named "City Road" and soon became choked with booths and amusements, and taverns with names such as "City of Moscow" and "The Free and Easy on the Ice." Goods were pedalled with the written tag that proclaimed they were "bought on the Thames." A sheep was roasted and sold by the slice as "Lapland Mutton." An elephant was led across the river below Blackfriars Bridge. There was even a book printed on the ice – *Frostiana: or A History of the River Thames in a Frozen State.* Many sketches and paintings were done of the festivities occurring on the frozen Thames.

It was to be the last Frost Fair on the Thames, but no one there knew this. It lasted for only a few days and then there was a thaw and the tides shifted the great slabs of ice and they drifted as floes down the Thames.

As the Fair was literally breaking up, nine men were left to guard one of the on-ice public houses. Most of the alcohol had been removed already, but the men drank the last of the gin that remained there. They fell asleep in the booth and when they awoke in the night their patch of ice had broken free and was floating fast through the river darkness. One of the men had the idea of starting a fire so they would be able to see the surroundings, but the flames quickly leapt out of control and set fire to the booth. Now the men were hurtling through the river darkness on a flaming ice island. They managed to hurl themselves into a lighter boat that had been torn from its moorings and was drifting past their island, but the lighter hit the piers of the Blackfriars Bridge and was dashed to pieces. The men were able to cling to the piers of the bridge and haul themselves, exhausted, up to safety.

The frozen Thames was not such a rarity in 1814 as it had been in earlier times. The freezing of the river was not a singular event in people's lives. They had memories of other freezings, other Frost Fairs.

Even the animals were becoming used to the frozen state of the river. On the last day of the Frost Fair, people watched as four donkeys crossed, by themselves, on the ice road that joined one side of the Thames to the other.

1820

—

The man is walking with his dog along the tow path by the river at Kew. Only yesterday he had been walking on the river ice, but it had unseated itself in the night and today the Thames is littered with ice floes and is too unstable to stand on.

Ice forms in secret and dissolves in secret. The man has been witness to the river freezing twice before, and each time he watched for the moment when the ice unhinged, and each time he somehow missed it. *It is like the dying*, he thinks now, walking along the tow path after his dog. *The dying wait until you leave the room before they will let themselves die.* Some acts are not for witnessing and perhaps the river covering and uncovering herself is one of these.

The dog has run on ahead, nosing some scent to earth, and the man has to trot to keep up with him. As they round a bend in the river they hear shouting and both stop, look up, and see a woman on her hands and knees on an ice floe, bobbing and spinning out on the surface of the river.

She is screaming for help, down on all fours like an animal bawling at the slaughter.

The ice floc is tippy. From the shore the man can see how it is tilting first one way and then another in the river's current. Every time the woman moves to stabilize herself she throws the balance off and the platform of ice where she is crouching threatens to slide her into the water.

"Stay put," yells the man, and begins to run along the bank, keeping pace with the floating woman.

"Stay there."

The dog runs along the bank as well, ahead of the man and barking excitedly.

"Help *me*," screams the woman.

The man knows that the water is too cold for him to be able to swim out to her and pluck her from the ice pan. He would freeze before he could reach her. He wants to save the woman, but he doesn't want to kill himself in the attempt. He looks frantically along the tow path. What he needs is a long stick or a rope, something he can use to throw or hold out to the distressed woman.

But there is nothing. There is nothing and the man is getting breathless from running along the bank. He is not a young man, is not used to going at such a pace.

"Help me," cries the woman, and then there is another cry, from farther up the river. The man turns and sees another woman, this one standing on another ice floe, legs far apart like a sailor balancing on the deck of a sloping ship.

"Help me," she yells.

The dog stops barking. The man stops running. He rubs his eyes to make sure he isn't imagining what he thinks he sees. He isn't. There are two separate women floating on two separate plates of ice down the river.

The first woman is almost past him now, and the man can't wait any longer. There won't be any other instrument of rescue besides his own body. He throws off his coat and stumbles to the water's edge. The cold of the river is so strong that it knocks him down when he struggles into the shallow water off the bank. He can't breathe, sitting in the cold of the river, water lapping at his chest.

And while he forces air back into his frozen lungs and pushes himself backwards and out of the river, both women topple from their ice floes and disappear into the Thames.

Later the man will find out that both of the drowned women were named Heather, and that they did not know one another. But now he sits on the bank, sputtering for breath and rubbing the feeling back into his legs. He cannot believe that he was unable to do anything, that it all happened so quickly and he was no help at all to those women. He sits there until his dog nudges him in the back of the neck and he remembers to get up and start walking, remembers how to save himself.

1880

——

The girl wakes to darkness and birdsong. She lies in her bed, eyes closed, and listens to the sweet music that slides just ahead of morning. The blankets are tucked up to her chin, only her nose and forehead are exposed to the cold air of the bedroom. It is still too early for rising and, if the girl keeps her eyes fast shut, she can imagine that she is waking up in a spring meadow, not in the middle of a frigid London winter.

The girl lies very quietly, so as not to wake her sisters who sleep on either side of her. Smallest in the centre, that is the edict in their house. She feels cozy with her big sisters close in beside her, each of them breathing the slow, heavy breath of sleep. She listens to the bird and feels like she is in a nest, that she is a baby bird waiting for the mother to return to her with food. The bird sounds so close, and when the girl opens her eyes, there it is, perched on the bedpost at the bottom of the bed.

The winter has been so cold that all manner of trees and shrubs have perished. Hollies that were well over a hundred years old have died, as have peach trees, also older than any living man. Rabbits that are starving have started to eat the oil and grease from machinery in the rail yards. The Thames has frozen over. Birds have begun to freeze to death, particularly that small symbol of spring, the Robin Redbreast, and instead of allowing this to happen, the people of England have taken the birds into their houses so that they may shelter there until spring returns.

In the girl's house there are two robins. They have built a nest on the roofbeam near the fireplace and they flutter about all day, gathering hair and bits of straw to furnish their little house. The girl's mother is constantly swatting at them as they fly low over her when she is cooking. It was not her idea to let the robins into the house. The girl's father, who worked at the rail yard, had come home one night with the story of the rabbits eating the grease from the trains. He was the one who mentioned the birds.

"It seems that people are letting the Robin Redbreast take shelter in their houses," he said. "To spare them this killing cold."

His daughters immediately supported this idea, and the mother's cries of protest were overwhelmed by the enthusiasm of the girls. It was not hard to find two frozen robins, huddled in the cave of their cold feathers on a stone wall near the railway station. The girl's father carried the birds home in his coat pockets – one in each pocket. For the first day they hunched miserably together on top of a doorframe, but the heat of the house soon revived their spirits and now they fly about quite happily. The girl leaves out bread for them and bits of fat from the supper meat. Sometimes they swoop down and pick things from the table – a rind of apple, a piece of cheese – while the mother shrieks and bats at them with a tea towel. The girl thinks they enjoy this and sometimes do it for their own pleasure, not because they are hungry. She likes to watch them flicker about the room, bathe in the basin of water that sits on the table at the end of her bed and is for washing her face in the morning.

"Well, well," said her father, when he first saw the nest on the roofbeam. "They seem to have made themselves quite at home."

The girl cannot wait until there are eggs in the nest, and then the little heads of the baby birds leaning up, mouths agape, chirping for food. The adult robins don't like to be touched, will not land on her finger, even though she has stood dead still for hours in the centre of the parlour with her finger extended. But the babies might be more easily tamed. The girl is hoping for this, hoping that the baby robins will want to stay with her even after the spring is here and the doors will be opened so the birds may leave the houses and be free again.

The girl looks at the robin on her bedpost, and he cocks his head and looks back at her. Somewhere downstairs the other robin is singing. All over London, the girl thinks, all over London this very same thing is happening. Each house is a dark lantern, and each one holds the lit flicker of bird within its ribs.

1895

—

This was the winter of the twelve-week frost. From the end of December to the middle of March the whole of England was plunged into bitterly cold weather. For a week in February the Thames was completely blocked by huge ice floes, some of them as much as seven feet thick. The non-tidal sections of the river froze solid. Horsedrawn coaches crossed the Thames at Oxford, and on the ice at Kingston there was a carnival,

topped off with the ceremonial roasting of an ox.

Ships were frozen into their moorings and the lightermen weren't able to land to off-load their cargo. On the Grand Surrey Canal between Rotherhithe and the Old Kent Road, crews of men were dispatched to break the ice so the coal supplies could travel their usual river route. The ice the men broke and threw up onto the banks formed an enormous ice wall, ten feet high and two miles long.

It was a winter with little snow, and skating was enjoyed on all the rivers and canals. A pond in Yorkshire froze all the way to the bottom.

This winter was as cold as the winter of 1814, and yet there was to be no Frost Fair on the ice of the Thames because the nature of the river had been changed by the destruction of the old London Bridge and the building, in 1831, of the new one. Where the old bridge had numerous arches and starlings to impede the flow of the Thames, the new bridge, designed by John Rennie, had only five arches and the water moved quicker and freer through those arches. The river was also being dredged at this time and the deepening of the channel strengthened the ebb and flow of the tides. The Thames was simply moving too swiftly to freeze where it had frozen in the past. The new bridge did not work as a dam, the way the old bridge had, and the Thames would never, will never, freeze solid in the heart of London again.

The story begins on the frozen Thames. *Suddenly the sun...* A young nobleman meets a Russian princess on the ice during a Frost Fair in the reign of Queen Elizabeth I. He is entranced by the princess, by the spectacle of the wonders on the ice. They skate together. *For some time, her silence...* The young nobleman has an open and unguarded heart. He is a poet, moved ardently by his own words and feelings, given quickly to love.

& when the sun dropped below the horizon... on an evening like this... He is besotted with the Russian princess, declares his passionate love for her without fear or hesitation. This happens as the evening is ending, with rockets being sent up into the night sky, to *shake out their petals (the image was Orlando's) as they reached the darkness.*

Orlando and Sasha will be separated in the novel, not just by culture and language, but also by centuries. This is a story that thaws the imagination, sets it spinning along a swift current of words. The novelist is playful and serious. She writes these words. She crosses them out. The book is written with an ease and quickness that she has never experienced before, and will never experience again. When she writes of Orlando, looking back through hundreds of years and remembering his love for Sasha, it is as though she is also recounting her own experience in writing the book.

love & the ice... & her veins had sung... in that white world like fire.

AUTHOR'S NOTE

—

This book is intended as a long meditation on the nature of ice. Each story is a story of transformation, as ice itself is the result of a transformative process. Because of climate change, brought on by the buildup of greenhouse gases in the atmosphere, we are in danger of losing ice from our world. If ice disappeared, we would not only lose the thing itself and its stabilizing place in the balance of nature, but we would also lose the idea of ice from our consciousness, and all the ways in which we are able to imagine it.

The dictionary quoted in these pages is Samuel Johnson's dictionary.

The italicized passages in the postscript are deleted lines from the first draft of Virginia Woolf's *Orlando*. These lines never made it into the final version of the book.

Most of the incidents referred to in *The Frozen Thames* are based on documented events. I am particularly grateful for the following three books: *Frost Fairs on the Thames* by Edward Walford; *Famous Frosts and Frost Fairs* by William Andrews; and, *Frostiana: or A History of the River Thames in a Frozen State* by G. Davis.

For Valerie Ashford
and in memory of Elizabeth Ashford

———

Acknowledgements

Further to the books mentioned in the Author's Note, I am grateful to *Frost Fairs on the Frozen Thames* by Nicholas Reed, and *Frosts, Freezes and Fairs* by Ian Currie.

Information regarding the frozen state of the Thames has been obtained through various meteorological sources, most notably The Met Office in the UK.

The lines from the first draft of *Orlando* are used with permission from The Society of Authors, who represent the literary estate of Virginia Woolf.

Information regarding Bess of Hardwick's household inventories was taken from *Of Household Stuff: The 1601 Inventories of Bess of Hardwick*, published by The National Trust.

The rhyme describing the death of Doll the apple-woman on page 114 is attributed to John Gay.

The gravestone inscription on page 134 is from a cemetery in Dorset, England.

The recipe for Jugged Hare is based on Hannah Glasse's version in *The Art of Cookery*, 1747.

I am grateful to the Environment Canada Library for allowing me access to *Frostiana: or A History of the River Thames in a Frozen State*.

I would like to thank the Banff Centre for the Arts, where this book was begun; and The Canada Council for financial support while it was being written. As always, I am grateful to my agent, Frances Hanna. And I would like to thank my editor, Susan Renouf, for her enthusiasm and her care.

Image Credits

186

IN years gone by, when there was
other journals which, by the use o
to the diffusion of useful knowled
speculate in the production of lar
which were so striking as to meet
Most of these prints will be foun
Illustrated " Pennant " (both in th
curious of these engravings is t
There are, in addition to the " live
the Great Frost of Charles II.'s r
completely blocked up with huge
" Temple-street," as the row of te
this view an ox is being roasted w
ward ; the frost of 1789, when t
and that of 1814, when the same r

Besides the three great Frosts, 1
refer engravings of displays of fir